Shadow Road

Present Day
Anne Damiano
Maria De Costa's Kitchen
Columbia, Maryland

"I went to medical school on a dare." Anne leaned back in her chair to watch her niece's response.

Maria's look of disbelief was obvious. "Really? I'd love to hear the rest of *that* story." She placed a tray of cookies on the table.

Anne glanced out the window. Trees tossed around in the driving rain. She shivered, thinking of the drive to Swan Cove. "It won't be tonight. Getting across the Bay Bridge is going to be a challenge if the storm gets much worse."

"What brought you to town today?"

"A short visit with some friends."

"Anyone I know?"

Anne nodded. "Connor Quinlan and I met with another old friend."

Maria's hand stopped in mid-air. She almost dropped the cup of coffee she was handing to her Aunt Anne. "THE CIA Connor Quinlan?"

"The one and only." Anne chuckled.

"How on earth would I know him?"

"You've known him since you were a little girl. He's almost always at the Fitzgerald family functions. He was at Mary-Katherine's wedding, as well as Brittany's baptism."

"Connor Quinlan is part of my best friend's family?"

"He's Mary-Katherine's uncle."

Maria slapped the heel of her hand against her forehead. "He's Mary-Katherine's Uncle Connor."

"Fraid so."

"Did you get to be friends with him when you worked for the CIA?"

Anne shook her head. "I've known Connor for a long time. We've been friends since sandbox days."

"Sandbox? You mean like – little-kid-sandbox?"

Anne's smile spread into a grin. "Sort of – Our sandbox was the beach in Lavallette. The Damianos, Quinlans, and Fitzgeralds all had summer homes on Virginia Avenue. The DeCosta beach house was about two blocks away. Our mothers were long-time friends. We were in and out of one another's houses every day, all summer long."

Maria pointed to a tray of wedding cookies. "Have some dessert, Aunt Anne." She picked up one of the sweets and took a bite. Powdered sugar sprinkled the front of her sweater.

Anne reached for a cookie and took a sip of coffee.

Maria smiled. "By all accounts, Connor Quinlan is quite a guy."

"Good way to describe Connor." A pang of regret radiated through Anne. "Just for the record, we did work together when I was in the CIA. He was part of the reason they recruited me."

"Really?" Maria looked both surprised and doubtful. "Tell me about it."

"About two years after I finished my psychiatry residency, I worked at a clinic in Georgetown…"

"Psych residency? But - you're a Public Health doc." Maria tried to brush the sugar from her sweater. "What other mysteries are hidden in your past?"

"Mysteries?"

Maria nodded; eyebrows raised. "You said you went to medical school on a dare. Then you became a psychiatrist. I didn't know anything about that stuff."

"You were just a little girl when all that happened. My life has been a bit unusual. Lots of twists and turns I never expected. Neither did anyone else for that matter. When I was growing up, I knew I wanted to take care of sick people. So, I went to Rutgers College of Nursing and worked as a nurse for about seventeen years. Many of the doctors I worked with bugged me to go to medical school. Finally, one of the physicians told me I didn't have the courage to go to medical school."

Maria giggled. "Sounds like he knew all the right buttons to push."

"He did." Anne laughed. "I did my first residency in Psychiatry. I gave that up a long time ago. The story's complicated."

"I'd love to hear it."

Gloria Casale

Rain and wind rattled the windows.

"I've got to get to the Eastern Shore before the weather gets much worse. We'll save that story for another day."

1989
Connor
Early March
Panama City, Panama

Connor, eager to get to Ft. Amador, scanned the deserted street. Darkened storefronts, broken windows, and shot-out streetlamps stretched the length of the avenue. Ft. Amador glowed in the distance.

He paused under the single undamaged streetlight.

Five men converged on him from a dark alley. One snarled and tossed a knife from hand to hand with skill and ease. "You got no business here, Yanqui."

Noriega's thugs.

The man closest to him grabbed his left arm. The leader's sneer turned into a smirk of impending victory. He raised his arm. The knife blade flashed.

Connor crouched, sprang, and struck the base of the man's nose with the heel of his right hand. Blood gushed down the thug's face leaving black streaks on his redshirt. His knife clanged to the pavement.

A kick from Connor sent the knife skidding out of the lamplight.

Two of the thugs grabbed his right arm. A third man grabbed Connor's feet. The fourth man body-slammed him from behind. Pain flashed through Connor's shoulder; his right arm fell useless at his side. He pulled his arm tight against his body. *Holy Mother of God, how'm I going to get out of this one?* The thought was half prayer, half hopeless reality.

The men pushed Connor against an abandoned storefront. One leaned his forearm against Connor's neck to hold him, immobile, against the rough brick wall. The thug licked his lips. A grin of victory slowly spread across his face. "Victor, check on Paco," he called over his shoulder. "I'll take care of this one."

Sudden bright lights illuminated the scene. A vehicle roared toward them.

The man holding Connor released his grip and retreated a few steps.

Connor resisted the urge to slide to the ground.

Gloria Casale

The jeep skidded to a stop. Two US military policemen jumped out.

A tall, well-muscled man with sergeant stripes on his sleeve strode toward Connor. His name tag declared him to be 'Jackson.' A no-nonsense stance removed any doubt that he was in charge. "You an American, Sir?"

"I am, Sergeant." Connor's voice was little more than a whispered croak.

Jackson caressed his holstered .45 automatic with his left hand and waved a substantial flashlight toward the thugs. "Vamoose, amigos."

The four men disappeared into the alley without a backward glance at the man on the pavement.

"Looks like we got here just in time. What brings you to this part of town?"

"Must've made a wrong turn. I was on my way to Ft. Amador."

"This isn't a good place to be at any time of the day or night." Jackson picked up the knife and whistled. "This is a significant pig sticker. You okay, Sir?"

Connor shook his head. "Don't think so. I'm pretty sure they dislocated my shoulder."

"We can get you to Ft. Amador in twenty minutes." Jackson nodded toward the distant lights. He folded the knife and put it in his pocket. "Webster, assist this gentleman into the jeep."

Webster crab-walked Connor to the jeep and hefted him into the passenger seat.

Jackson eased himself behind the wheel, "Hop in the back, Webster." He gunned the motor and swung the jeep in a U-turn.

Connor grabbed the dashboard with his left hand and held his breath. Pain shot through his shoulder to his neck and back. "Glad you did."

"You're lucky we made one last sweep, Sir."

"Dignity battalions and Panamanian Defense Forces prowl this section of town lookin' for American GIs. They hate us."

The jeep bumped over the rutted road. Every jolt sent another flash of pain through Connor's shoulder.

"We'll be at the medical facility in about twenty minutes."

Connor gave a quick headshake. "I need to get to the Embassy or Ft. Clayton – whichever's closest."

"You got it. Ft. Clayton base hospital, Sir."

"Not the hospital – G2."

"G2, Sir?" Jackson pushed down on the accelerator. "SWEET JESUS!" he muttered, "I JUST PICKED ME UP A SPOOK."

Connor
New York City
April 16, 1989

Connor Quinlan entered the corridor leading to his office at One World Trade Center. He knuckle-rapped his Secretary's desk. "Good morning, Angela."

"Good morning, Mr. Quinlan. His secretary jumped up and followed a step behind. She plopped the day's schedule on his desk. "What did the doctor say?"

"He said my shoulder's healing well."

"And?"

Connor bit his lower lip. He knew Angela's questions would continue but he couldn't resist goading her. "And what?"

"And," her voice reflected her impatience, "what *else* did the doctor say?"

Connor's voice took on an impatient tone. "About what you'd expect. I have to be careful. The shoulder could dislocate again." Connor laughed. "I guess I'll have to give up my dream of being a tennis star."

"Fat chance of that. When did *you* ever play tennis?" Angela pointed at the schedule. "You've got a couple of busy days coming up."

He glanced down the list. "So, what else is new?"

Angela sighed, her shoulders drooped. "Mr. Killeen called about an hour ago. He wants you to call him back immediately."

Connor nodded and dialed Killeen's number.

"My office. ASAP." Killeen clicked off.

Connor stood and grabbed a pre-packed suitcase from the closet. Pain shot through his right shoulder. He shifted the bag to his left hand and started toward the door.

"Where do you think you're going?" Angela tried to block the door, feet wide apart hands on her hips. "You have a full schedule of appointments this afternoon. And your meeting with the commissioner starts tomorrow morning at ten."

"Make excuses. Cancel my appointments. Have Jim Walker cover the meeting for me."

Connor
Four Hours Later
Washington, DC

Connor stepped out of the Amtrak train at Union Station. He lingered at a newsstand for a few minutes, selected a newspaper, then pretended to check out the florist stand near the exit.

When he was sure no one was following him, he tossed a few dollars into the hat of a saxophonist on his way out of the building.

Connor walked down the hill, crossed Massachusetts Avenue, and checked into the Phoenix Park Hotel. The hotel and the Dubliner Pub commanded the entire corner of F Street and North Capitol. Irish décor graced the inside and exterior of both establishments.

He booked a room with one of his alternate IDs, left his bag with the bell captain, then hailed a taxi. "The J.W. Marriott, please."

The cabbie drove with reckless abandon through the busy streets and pulled into the apron of the Marriott.

Connor paid the fare in cash, walked into the hotel, and took the elevator to the convention center level. He walked the length of the second floor and exited the massive building on Massachusetts Avenue. After a short walk to the Carnegie Library, he hailed another cab.

"Where to, sir?"

"The Floriana Restaurant, Seventeenth Street. It's pretty close to DuPont Circle."

"Yes, sir," the cabbie replied, setting his timer, "I know it well."

Massachusetts Avenue was ablaze with color. Bright purple pansies, yellow daffodils, and rows of red and white flowering shrubs lent brilliant color to the manicured entrances of each Embassy. Their national flags flew straight and proud in the brisk wind.

Connor had a significant hike from DuPont Circle to Killeen's office. He intentionally selected a random route. He strolled through the neighborhoods and reversed direction several times. Finally, Connor approached a gray stone townhouse and pressed the doorbell.

Within seconds a loud click released the lock.

Gloria Casale

To the left of the entrance, a large room held a couch and chairs that faced a fireplace. An afternoon soap opera played on the TV. To a casual viewer, the space appeared to be an upper-middle-class living room. The electronics attached to the blinds, drapes, lights, and TV coordinated to convince a casual observer that someone lived there.

Connor started down the long hall leading from the foyer to the rear of the townhouse. Halfway down the hall, he opened a door on the right and peeked in. The room held state of the art surveillance equipment. A muscular, dark-skinned man and a tall, thin, blond woman sat at a bank of computers. A barely discernible flicker of their eyelids acknowledged Connor. They concentrated on the bevy of computer screens.

He closed the door and continued to Killeen's office.

Ornate brass andirons rested on the hearth. Multi-paned windows overlooked a secluded courtyard.

Killeen reflected the build and demeanor of a military man used to command. All the papers on his desk were in neat piles. The window blinds were open to a precise angle. Order and routine ruled Killeen's life.

The office retained the charm and artistry from a previous era. Mahogany panels and wainscoting covered the walls. Amber torchiers graced the massive mantle of the cobalt blue-tiled fireplace.

Connor helped himself to coffee from a side table. "From the look of this place, you must be upsetting television reception for a half a mile."

Killeen shook his head. "They tell me it's all shielded, and no signals leave the building. We haven't had any complaints from our neighbors. Besides, I'm sure everyone in this neighborhood has cable." The man motioned to an overstuffed gray tweed chair in front of his desk. "Good to see you. How's the shoulder?"

Anne
The Institute
Georgetown, DC
The Same Day

Anne rubbed the back of her neck to relieve the muscle spasm and tension. Her day had been long and intense.

Anne's medical school diploma and board certification hung behind her desk. The right sidewall held one of Anne's photographs, 'Sunset on Swan Cove.' The picture had been enlarged, printed on canvas, and artfully framed. A soft, knit throw, draped over the single armchair, picked up the subtle shades of pale green and lavender reflected in the water of Swan Cove.

Helena Empañada had been Anne's last patient of the day.

Six years ago, when Helena's mother died, her father sent her to a convent in South America. Last September, she started her university studies at Trinity College in Washington.

Seventeen-year-old Helena had been innocent until a few months before. On New Year's Day, a brutal rapist attacked her during a visit to her father's plantation.

A private jet dressed out with a complete hospital room, and a three-member medical team, brought Helena to Georgetown Medical Center.

Gynecological surgeons repaired Helena's physical damage. After a ten-day recovery, the medical team at Georgetown chose Anne to help the young woman work through her emotional scars.

Anne's office phone rang.

Señor Empañada's phone calls always came minutes after the girl left Anne's office. Helena's father was a stern and authoritative man, with well-known connections to the drug cartels. He was anxious to have his beautiful, well-mannered daughter return home. The man obsessed over his daughter's progress and demanded the impossible. "Helena has not responded to your treatment. I need her on the plantation. She has duties to fulfill."

Anne took a deep breath and slowly exhaled before she responded. "Señor, counseling takes time. Helena had significant physical and emotional trauma. Please understand. Repairing the emotional damage takes time."

"I warn you, Dr. Damiano, I'm an impatient man. She did not come home for Spring Break. I expect her to come to Columbia when this semester ends."

"I will certainly try to help her accept a return to Columbia. But she hasn't resolved the fear resulting from the trauma she experienced during her last visit."

"Helena has nothing to fear on my plantation. No man will dare come near her again. I've made sure of that."

Anne heard several clicks, then a dial tone. She rubbed her forehead and carefully placed the phone receiver in its cradle.

Anne
The Same Evening

Bone-tired, Anne walked home, ready for an evening of rest. Today's patients were among her most challenging. Ronnie, the psychopathic product of an overbearing mother and an absentee father. Lionel, the poor little rich boy with parents who'd coddled him, and never taught him responsibility.

The threatening phone call from Helena's father put the exclamation mark on her day.

As Anne closed and locked her front door, her phone rang. She stared at the phone. Months of annoying and frightening calls prompted her to get an unlisted number.

Who could be calling? They just changed the number yesterday.

The shrill ring persisted.

It's probably just a wrong number. Anne grabbed the receiver. "Hello?"

"I've missed you, Wiggles."

Her breath caught at the sound of the familiar voice. "Connor?"

"The one and only." His deep baritone voice carried a hint of laughter.

She took a breath, both pleased to hear from him and angry that it had been so long since his last call. "It's been a while."

"I've been out of the country," his voice turned serious. "Just got back. I'd like to take you out for dinner tonight."

Anne felt her cheeks burn. "Tonight?" She looked at the sheaf of faxed messages waiting for her attention. "Tomorrow would be better. I've…"

"I need to see you." He paused. "Eight o'clock at the Sea Catch. I'll meet you there." The connection clicked off before she could refuse.

Anne slammed the receiver in the cradle. *I guess it's easy to access an unlisted number if you're a CIA operative. Dinner?* She shook her head. *We'll have a great dinner. He'll stay here for the night. Then he'll disappear again.*

Anne glanced at his picture and sighed.

The clock in the vestibule donged seven.

Who am I kidding?

I have just enough time to shower and change if I'm going to get to the restaurant by eight.

She ran up the stairs and kicked off her shoes. One rolled toward the closet, and the other was half under the bed. Anne pulled off her clothes and left them in a tangle on the floor.

He appears. He disappears. He can't tell me where he's going, where he's been, or – whatever. Anne shook her head and turned on the shower.

She adjusted the water temperature and tried to suppress a smile.

"Oh, Connor," she sighed, stepping into the shower, "I haven't seen you in months – what's with the urgency of seeing you tonight?" She squirted shampoo onto her hair and rubbed it into a thick lather.

Anne tried to relax the muscles in the neck and back under the cascade of hot water

Anne
Forty Minutes Later

Anne, dressed in a black silk sheath, diamond stud earrings, and a smile, locked the front door of her townhouse and hurried down the steps.

At five minutes to eight, she walked across the brick-paved courtyard toward the double doors of the Sea Catch.

The restaurant had its usual Friday night crowd. People were lined four-deep along the Raw Bar. Toward the rear of the room, two bartenders worked at top speed to fill orders from the waitresses and the patrons sitting at the bar.

Anne slipped through the crush of bodies hoping to spy Connor. *Maybe this time I'll spy Connor before he sees me. It would be great if I could pull that off – just once.*

She suddenly felt a hand on her waist. "You look beautiful, Sweetheart," Connor whispered and guided her toward the balcony door. "We'll be eating outside tonight."

As they moved across the room, an older woman approached Anne.

"Excuse me, aren't you Doctor Damiano?" the woman asked.

Connor faded into the crowd.

"Yes. How did you know?"

"I saw your picture in The Washingtonian."

Anne smiled at the woman.

"Would you sign my menu?"

"I'd be glad to Mrs....?"

"Oh! Wilson. Jane Wilson." The woman handed her a menu and rummaged through her purse. "My daughter is going to be *so* jealous. I can't wait to tell her I met you." With a smile of victory, she handed a pen to Anne.

"I hope the management doesn't find out that you're stealing one of their menus," Anne teased.

"I'll hide it in my bag," the woman giggled and gestured to her purse.

"Good meeting you." Anne turned and started to walk toward the patio doors.

Connor materialized out of the crowd and opened the door for her.

"How do you manage to appear and disappear at will?"

"Training, my dear. Long years of training and necessity."

Miguel

Miguel entered the restaurant a few seconds after Anne. Luis followed behind. They leaned against one end of the bar, watched Anne's progress through the room, and saw Connor open the door for her.

Miguel nodded toward Anne and Connor. "Is that who I think it is?"

Luis blinked at the mass of people in the restaurant. His gaze shifted from one group to another.

Miguel pointed. "Over there – by the balcony door."

Luis shrugged his shoulders and shook his head. "The broad? We followed her here. Just like the boss ordered."

"Not her. The guy with her."

"So – she met a friend for dinner. Who cares?"

"The guy looks like Quinlan."

Luis blinked and refocused for a few seconds. "Yeah, he does. Why's the doc with Quinlan?"

Miguel's lips pulled into a downward pout. "Don' know."

They watched Connor open the patio door to usher Anne onto the deck.

"From the way he's lookin' at her, she's not a business associate." Miguel lifted his chin and puckered his lower lip. "The boss'll want to know about this." He reached into his pocket and brought out several quarters. "Give him a call." He handed the quarters to Luis. "Tell the boss we found Quinlan. And let him know Quinlan's with Helena's doctor."

Luis slid off the stool. "Save my drink." He took the proffered quarters from Miguel and walked out the front door.

Connor

Connor guided Anne to a table at the far end of the patio. He sat with his back against the gray stone wall of the restaurant. Hurricane lamps on each table lent a golden glow to the patio. A faint breeze rustled the leaves of the ancient trees that lined the canal. The earthy smell of the moss growing along the water's edge mingled with the scent of flowers.

Anne smiled, thankful to be away from the noisy chatter inside the restaurant.

Connor leaned back, allowing his muscles to relax. All the tension and anger of the past few hours melted away.

Anne sat in the chair to his left.

The Sea Catch balcony, with its rough-hewn planks and rustic balustrade, was the perfect venue for a quiet dinner. The canal, a vestige of Georgetown's past, offered a quiet corridor through the bustling city.

"Cocktails?" Their waiter pulled a pen from his shirt pocket.

"Yes, please." Anne gave the man a mischievous smile. "The gentleman will have a Tanqueray Martini, shaken not stirred, with a twist."

"And the lady will have a Bloody Mary with the slightest dash of tabasco, go easy on the vodka," Connor chimed in.

The waiter chuckled. "Sounds like you two have done this before."

"Aye, we have," Connor affected a Scottish burr.

Their lobster dinners were delicious. And, the wine Connor selected complimented the food.

"Where are you off to now?" Anne toyed with her fork. She pushed a bite of cheesecake across her plate.

Connor shrugged, "They haven't told me. I'll find out tomorrow." He ate the last bite of his dessert. "Coffee and Sambuca?"

"Of course. Wouldn't seem right to forego our tradition."

He signaled the waiter. "We'll have our coffee now, and sambuca, please."

The waiter served the anise-flavored liqueur en flambé.

When the flame died out, Anne swirled the coffee beans and gestured to Connor.

He raised his glass. "To Belleville."

"To Garwood," she said in response.

"And long, lazy summer days on the beach in Lavallette," they chorused.

He sighed, then drained his glass.

Anne looked up. "What's with the big sigh?"

"Thoughts about a simpler time. I miss the good old days. I miss the shore."

"I miss the Jersey shore, too. The good old days?" She laughed. "We sound like two ninety-year-olds. 'Dearie, do you remember when'....," she sang.

Connor slipped payment into the leather presenter. "Those days are gone forever, I'm afraid."

"Are you staying at the J.W. Marriott?"

He shook his head. "The Park Hotel."

"It's a bit of Irish flavor you're wantin' tonight?"

Connor chuckled. "Why not? Danny Coleman made the pub and hotel reminiscent of the 'ould sod.'"

The candle flame flickered as his hand moved to cover hers. He nodded toward the steps. "Let's take the footpath."

Neither spoke as they walked down the staircase and turned toward Thirty-first Street on the dark, secluded path. His arm eased around her waist. At the old canal turnstile, she moved into his arms and tilted her head up.

Connor kissed her and pressed a folded paper into her hand, "Hold tight to the note. Don't open it 'till you get home. Burn it after you read it. Flush the ashes down the toilet."

Anne's brow wrinkled. She nodded and slid the note into her purse.

When they reached Thirty-first Street, Connor hailed a cab, gave the cabbie Anne's address, and handed him a twenty-dollar bill.

One last kiss and a soft 'I love you.' He opened the door to the cab, gave her a rueful smile, and waited for her to slide into the back seat. He carefully closed the door and blew a kiss to her before the cab pulled away.

Gloria Casale

Anne

Anne slid out of the taxi and climbed the half story of brick stairs. When she reached the landing, she turned. The cab was gone. A black sedan idled in the middle of the narrow street.

She unlocked the heavy oak door and slipped inside, secured the deadbolt, and turned off the front light. Then she switched on the hall light and pulled the note from her purse.

Anne ~ In a week or two, I may need a safe haven. Would it be possible for me to use the cottage at Swan Cove?
If you agree, walk to the back of the house and turn on the kitchen light. Wait ten minutes, turn off the kitchen light, and turn the light on in your office. Leave your desk light on for just a few minutes, then continue your usual routine. If I have to use the cottage, you'll receive a dozen yellow roses. Do NOT come to the cottage while I'm there. You'll receive a spring bouquet when I leave. Destroy this note.

Anne walked down the hall to the kitchen, snapped on the light, and checked her watch. Her stomach clenched. She was unable to shrug off an uneasy feeling. She turned the gas on under the tea kettle and put a tea bag into a mug.

She lit a corner of Connor's note from the stove, allowed the ashes to fall into a saucer, then carried the plate to the small downstairs bathroom, and flushed the ashes. Back in the kitchen, the tea kettle whistled— Anne checked her watch. Seven minutes had passed since she turned on the kitchen light.

She poured hot water over the teabag and stirred in a teaspoon of sugar—thirty seconds to go. At precisely ten minutes, she snapped off the light and walked to her office.

Anne leaned over and turned on her desk lamp. She picked up Connor's picture and stared at it for a few minutes. "What's going on? What kind of danger are you dealing with?" She straightened a few piles of papers, then turned out the light and went upstairs.

Before turning on any lights, she walked to the guest bedroom, sidled next to a front window to view the street. A man sat in the passenger seat of the black car parked across the street. He flicked a smoldering cigarette butt onto the road.

Connor
The Next Morning
April 17, 1989

Connor stepped out of the elevator and scanned the hotel lobby. He dropped his room key card into the express check out and handed his bag to the red-jacketed bell captain. "I'll pick the bag up later today."

The bellman gave him a receipt and smiled. "Be sure to bring this with you, sir."

Connor scrutinized the street traffic and entry apron of the hotel.

Two men sat in the front seat of a car parked near the taxi queue. The passenger shot a glance at Connor, looked down, and nodded to the driver.

The doorman signaled for the next taxi and held the door open while Connor slid into the back seat. "Where to, Sir?" the cab driver asked.

"Dupont Circle." *They must have been parked there for hours.*

Connor slid across the seat and watched the vehicle in the rearview mirror. They *were waiting for me.*

The sedan inched into traffic a few cars behind the taxi.

Coincidence? Connor shook his head. He leaned forward. "I've changed my mind, driver. Take me to Metro Center."

Connor slid across the seat and used the side view mirror to keep an eye on the car.

When the cab turned on to Twenty-third Street, the sedan, two cars behind, made the same turn.

The cabbie slowed as he approached Metro Center.

"Thank you. Slow down a little more, but don't stop." In one smooth move, Connor dropped a twenty-dollar bill on the front seat and jumped from the taxi. He strode through the arched hall to the escalators and stepped onto the moving staircase.

At the bottom of the first level, Connor pretended to read the directions on a subway signpost. He studied the reflections in the glass.

When Connor was sure the passenger had enough time to find him, Connor rode down to the blue line platform. At the bottom, he turned and stepped onto the up escalator.

The guy was obvious. Connor pointed at him and smiled.

About forty years old. A little less than six feet tall. Pockmarked face, greasy black hair, and a thin mustache. He wore an ill-fitting dark brown jacket, lighter brown wrinkled slacks, and a yellow shirt.

The man glared.

You violated one of the first rules of surveillance, buddy. You made eye contact.

Connor strolled to the red line platform and waited for the next train.

When it pulled into the station, Connor waited for a beat, then stepped into the back of a crowded car. He watched his pursuer jump into the adjoining car and move to the center of the aisle.

Chimes signaled the door closing. Connor stepped off the train, then turned and waved as the train pulled out of the station.

Killeen
Thirty Minutes Later

Killeen looked at his watch and frowned. "You're late." He gestured toward the coffee pot. "We have some things to work out."

Connor shrugged and poured himself a cup. "I had to confuse a tail." He sipped the strong brew, then slumped into an overstuffed chair to give his muscles and nerves a chance to relax. "Did you put someone on me this morning?"

"I didn't. I don't think the boss did, either. Tell me about it."

Connor handed Killeen the receipt for his bag and recounted the morning's adventure.

Killeen reached for the phone. "Somebody followed Quinlan this morning. He lost him in the subway, but it's clear they know he's in town. Do you still want him to go?" He nodded and replaced the receiver, then pushed back from his desk. "Excuse me for a few minutes."

Connor gave a two-fingered salute and swung his feet onto a hassock.

Killeen left the room and climbed a flight of stairs. He entered the office directly above his. The man behind the desk had the same military bearing and fervor for tidiness as Killeen. Except for the color of the fireplace tiles and the fabrics, the two offices appeared identical. Forest green predominated the upstairs decor.

"Quinlan said two guys followed him from the hotel this morning. He lost them in the Metro."

"I'll check to see if they were friendly," the older man replied. "It's peculiar. I wonder how he was picked up." He paused and rubbed his chin. "Prepare a list of who knows he's here. Include the people from State who read into this mission." Then, with a look of concern. "How did Quinlan's shoulder check out?"

Killeen shrugged. "The doc said Quinlan's shoulder is okay. He'll be in pain for a while. What did they say at headquarters? Did Donovan say the CIA decided the attack in Panama was random?"

"They couldn't find anyone in Panama who might've blown his cover." The man shrugged. "Looks like the men who attacked Quinlan were Noriega thugs."

Killeen shook his head. "I'm not convinced. I don't know if the attack in Panama and this morning's event are associated, but I'm pretty sure we shouldn't rule it out."

"Doesn't make any difference. No choice. Quinlan's gotta go. We'll have to take that chance. He's the only one with the right contacts."

Killeen walked back down the stairs to his own office and sat in the easy chair Connor dubbed 'The Monsignor Killeen Chair.' Killeen used this chair when a situation demanded intense conversation. Most of the discussions conveyed bad news.

He gestured for Connor to sit in the chair opposite him. "You're going south again. Same as usual. No backup. Shallow cover. On this trip, you're simply an expert on international shipping law. The Panamanian businessmen have requested your expertise." He paused to allow Connor to process the information.

After a few beats, Connor nodded.

"We've arranged a contact who'll make sure you meet the right people and establish your cover. Her name is Paola Del Rubin. She's a Panamanian journalist. I think you've met her husband."

Connor tilted his head to the side and puckered his lips. "I've met Luis —I never met his wife. I'm surprised she didn't have to leave Panama. How come they never used her as bait? Noriega's pals wanted her husband to ship drugs. He refused. We were able to get Luis out of Panama and into a U.S. safe house before Noriega's men killed him."

"For the time being, Paola is safe. Noriega's people haven't been willing to go after her. She's a top journalist, beautiful, and very popular with the Panamanians. Even Noriega had to worry about the power of the press."

Killeen handed him a file containing all the necessary operational data.

Connor grabbed the file and retreated to a small adjacent office.

Gloria Casale

Anne
The Same Morning

Anne pushed open the door to the Institute, walked across the lobby, and smiled at her secretary. "Good Morning, Maggie. Sorry I'm late."

Maggie looked up and smiled. "Good Morning, Dr. Anne. No worries, you don't have any patients until this afternoon. It's been pretty quiet."

"Any calls?"

"No calls, but Dr. Smithfield stopped by about a half-hour ago. He wanted to know where you were."

Anne choked back a sour taste. *Will that man ever accept the fact that I don't want to have anything to do with him?*

Anne accepted a few dates with Herb when she first started working at the institute. He took her to openings at the opera, ballet, and philharmonic. They went to social events that were just stories in the Washington Times for most people. But the excitement dampened as he attempted to increase his control over her life.

"Did Dr. Smithfield say what he wanted?"

"Not really. He said something about being worried about you."

Anne's rubbed her forehead. "Worried about me?" *It's been more than a year since we stopped dating. He should have gotten the idea by now. His fixation is becoming pathologic.*

Maggie pursed her lips, shrugged her shoulders, and shook her head. She handed a pile of messages to Anne. "These came in this morning. You have an appointment at the University tomorrow."

Anne unlocked her office door, placed the messages next to her phone, and dropped her keys on the blotter. She leafed through the correspondence, hoping to find a message from Connor. His note suggested he was in grave danger.

A kernel of concern bloomed deep in her chest.

She picked up the phone and dialed the Park *Hotel*. Anne wondered why Connor stayed at the Park Hotel. He usually stayed at the J.W. Marriott. The thread of anxiety tightened.

"May I speak to Mr. Quinlan?"

"Just a moment, Ma'am." The line went silent. A few minutes later, the operator came back on the line. "There is no guest registered by that name."

"Please, check again. Mr. **Connor** Quinlan. He told me he'd be at the Park Hotel. He was quite specific."

"Our records indicate there has not been a guest here with name in the past week."

"Sorry, I must have misunderstood. Thank you." Anne gently placed the phone in the cradle. She called the J.W. Marriott and the Ana Hotel just to make sure. Neither hotel had any record of Mr. Quinlan staying there at any time in the past ten days. The tightness in her chest increased.

A tall, handsome man with auburn hair stormed into her office, leaned over her desk, and snarled, "Where were you last night?"

Anne looked up. "Where I was last evening is none of your business, Herb. I've made it quite clear that I don't want to have anything to do with you outside this office."

He waved his hand and raised his voice. "You're just being silly. I tried to call you several times. There's something wrong with your phone. I kept getting a message saying the number was disconnected."

"Stop shouting." Her voice acerbic, "I had my phone number changed. The new number is unlisted. The number you called is no longer in service."

"I went to your house. You didn't answer the door."

"I was out."

"What time did you get in?"

"None of your business."

"Who were you with?"

Anne glared. "Also, none of your business."

"I wanted to tell you that I'll pick you up at six-thirty tonight."

Anne reared back in her chair. "You'll what?"

"Six-thirty, on the dot. Be ready. We can't be late."

"What are you talking about? I have no intention of going anywhere with you."

"It's the opera season-opening night. They're performing The Magic Flute. Mumsie will be waiting for us at the Kennedy Center."

Anne vigorously shook her head. "Count me out. I have no desire to go to the opera tonight. I don't want to go anywhere with you." I have things to catch up on at home."

"Of course, you're going. Mumsie decided. She says it's time we introduced you to Georgetown Society."

Mumsie? Anne could feel the heat rising from her chest to her neck to her temples. Almost every weekend for the past month, Herb asked her out. She'd refused every invitation. "I said, **no**. I will **not** go to the opera tonight. I've told you to stop calling me. Stop bugging me. Where I go and what I do are **no** concern of yours."

"Of course, they are my concern. I need to know where the future Mrs. Herbert Jefferson Smithfield Junior is spending her time. Mumsie wants to talk to you about the engagement party. I need your new phone number. Mumsie also needs your mother's address."

"The future Mrs. Herbert Jefferson Smithfield, Junior? What are you talking about? I have no intention of becoming the future Mrs. Herbert Jefferson Smithfield, Jr."

"We can't disappoint Mumsie."

"Have you heard anything I've said? I'm not going to dinner with you tonight or any night. I thought I made that clear a year ago."

"Of course, you'll join us. Mumsie and I decided all of this yesterday."

"You and Mumsie decided? Are you listening to anything I've said?"

Despite the irritation in her voice, Herb persisted. "On second thought, be ready at six. I want to make sure you look respectable. Wear something formal. It **is** opening night, after all."

"Herb, I am NOT going to the opera with you tonight or **any** night." Anne's eyes narrowed. She ground her teeth. "We dated a few times last year. I told you I wasn't interested in seeing you again. My life is my own. I am not interested in dating you. I don't ever want to see you outside this office."

Herb walked around the desk and towered over her. "You're being silly. Mumsie is so looking forward to helping you make the wedding plans. I've already spoiled the best part of the evening. I wanted to save our announcement as a surprise for her. But I was just so excited. I had to tell her at breakfast this morning."

"Wedding plans? Announcement? What did you tell her at breakfast?"

Herb waved his hand. "She's been so anxious to start the wedding plans. I told her to go ahead."

"You what?"

Herb waved away her comment. "I put my place on the market yesterday. The movers are packing my apartment today. Most of my stuff will go in storage."

"Now, what are you talking about?"

"I'll bring a few things to your place, of course."

"Why would you bring **anything** to my townhouse?"

"I've already called the newspaper. The announcement of our nuptials will be in the weekend edition. We are adults – there's no sense in living apart."

"You've what? Nuptials? You are not moving into my townhouse."

"Mumsie approves. She's delighted we're getting married."

Anne could only stare - open-mouthed.

"I won't bring much. It will be just a few things. They'll make me feel more at home."

Anne jumped up. Her cheeks burned with repressed anger. "You're delusional!"

Herb recoiled.

"Get this straight. You will not move in with me. I will not go out with you tonight." Anne started toward the door. "I am *not* the future Mrs. Herbert Jefferson Smithfield, Junior."

He grabbed her arm and jerked her towards him. "There's someone else. Who is he?"

"Get your hands off me." Anne's voice dropped to low and threatening timbre.

"I demand to know."

"Get out of my office." She winced when she yanked her arm free. "Don't ever touch me again. Don't ever come into my office again. I'll call the police if you even come near me." Anne stormed out of her office.

Herb

Herb stared at the door. Then paced back and forth in front of Anne's desk.

She doesn't realize how much I love her. Someday, she'll know. Eventually, she'll understand. What if something happened to me?

He rubbed his forehead. "Maybe I should take an overdose of sleeping pills? Then she would realize how important I am."

Herb walked back to her desk and rifled through her phone messages.

Nothing here. "Anne **must** be seeing someone."

He noticed her keys.

She never would let me have a key to her place.

Herb slid the keys into his pocket.

Connor
Killeen's Office

Connor walked back into Killeen's office and dropped the file in a wire basket. "Wish me luck."

Killeen nodded. "Remember," he warned, "the Panamanian shippers think the only reason you're there is to answer their questions about maritime law and international port regulations. We need to know the business class mindset. Find out as much as you can. Find out if they support or oppose reinstating a legitimate government in Panama."

Connor pursed his lips and nodded.

"Your bag will be at the airport. We've added some clothes that are more suitable for Panama. They'll hand the bag to you at the ticket counter."

Connor nodded again.

"Don't assume anyone is friendly. If things heat up, get out as fast as you can." Killeen stood. "If your cover's blown, you'll be killed."

Connor
The Same Morning

From 1000 feet, Connor looked out of the aircraft window to watch the activity on the Bay of Panama. Freighters, container ships, and tankers rode at anchor, waiting their turn to pass through the Canal. The plane banked to the left. He caught a glimpse of fishing boats heading out to sea.

Commerce, the blood supply of the world's economy, passed through the ditch American engineers dug across the steaming Isthmus of Panama. The Canal converted Panama into a financial center. Billions of dollars passed through this small country, much of the money tainted by illegal drug commerce.

Familiar doubts ran through Connor's mind. *I wish* – A sarcastic chuckle.

Connor's seatmate frowned at him.

"Oh, sorry. Just thinking out loud."

The man seated beside him snapped open a magazine.

Yeah, I wish. If wishes were fishes, Connor chuckled at his mother's mantra.

Another caustic look from his seatmate.

Connor took a deep breath and straightened. *Anne and I can never be.* His mind snapped back to his assignment and its threats. *She'd be in constant danger.*

Fifteen minutes later, Connor walked down the dilapidated jetway into Torrijos International Airport. Numerous armed guards created a sense of foreboding. They walked in pairs, unsmiling.

A bored customs official asked a few questions, marked Connor's luggage, and waved him on.

Pain shot down Connor's arm when he grabbed his valise. It was a vivid reminder of his last visit to Panama. An all too familiar feeling of vulnerability settled in his gut.

Crowds of people filled the customs passageway. Chauffeurs held placards with names printed on them. Families craned their necks and chattered while they waited for relatives. Frequent outbursts of excited cries signaled the arrival of a loved one. Their enthusiasm added to the terminal's cacophony.

Connor scanned the crowd, then stepped out of the air-conditioned building. The tropical air wrapped him in a steamy wet blanket.

He paused for a few seconds and scanned the waiting line of vehicles. He started to walk toward the taxi queue.

A hand touched his left elbow. "Dr. Quinlan?"

Connor turned. An attractive woman watched him, quiet and composed.

"Señora Del Rubin?"

"Yes, I am Paola Del Rubin." She gestured toward a black limousine. "My driver is here. We will take you to your hotel."

A slight man dressed in black slacks and a white guayabera, the loose, decorative shirt favored by men in Central American countries, stood at parade rest near the back door of the limo.

"Please, allow Juan to help you with your luggage."

Connor handed his valise to the chauffeur. "Thank you."

Juan leaned over to put the bag in the trunk.

Connor could discern the outline of a weapon beneath the driver's shirt. Connor's eyebrows raised in a questioning look as he turned toward Señora Del Rubin.

She answered with a grim smile and a nod. "These are troubled times, Dr. Quinlan."

Juan opened the rear door, Paola slid into the back seat. The driver signaled Connor to sit beside her. Juan locked the door and pushed it shut. When he moved to the driver's seat, he turned the ignition and closed the privacy window between the front and back seat of the limo.

"I understand you can provide information relating to our maritime business concerns."

"Yes, more specifically, answering your questions regarding maritime law and how it relates to international port regulations."

"I took the liberty of arranging a dinner for this evening. There are a few people you should meet. I've also planned your schedule for the next few days."

Brightly colored buses, vendor carts, automobiles, and people clogged the streets. Juan skillfully drove through the busy thoroughfares.

Gloria Casale

The contrasts and inconsistencies of Panama made an impact on Connor with every visit. A bustling modern city, close to the jungle. The country moved up the ladder in Latin America's competitive economies. Still, the rural areas continued to fight dengue, malaria, and yellow fever.

"I have a message for you, Dr. Quinlan."

"A message?"

"Ora said he would like to have a short meeting with you."

Ora? Here? He's supposed to be in Europe. Connor studied Paola's face. Her expression friendly but bland.

Connor smiled. "Ora's an old friend. I haven't seen him in several years. Ora is his nickname. His last name is difficult for many people to pronounce."

"Mr. Oratchewski is an interesting man."

Her simple reply was sufficient. Paola had been read into the project. She could be trusted.

Connor smiled. "Please, call me Connor. We'll be working together for the next few days, at least. We should be on a first-name basis. And, you don't have to refer to me as 'Doctor Quinlan.'" In the States, attorneys are called 'Mister.'"

"But while you're in Panama, you'll be called doctor by most people."

The car pulled into the entrance drive to the hotel. A vast grassy area between the street and the hotel entrance caught Connor's attention.

An officious looking doorman opened the car door.

Connor stepped out of the car.

Paola extended her hand. "My publisher is hosting tonight's dinner. It will be a casual get together. The men will be wearing guayabera."

"That's good news." Connor hated the heat and humidity of Panama. The loose-fitting guayabera and slacks would be far more comfortable.

"We'll pick you up at eight."

Juan handed Connor's valise to the doorman, closed the rear door of the limo, and got back into the driver's seat.

Connor entered the hotel. Men wearing business suits filled the lobby. He wondered if they were Noriega's security people.

A hallway to the right of the entrance had a sign indicating the access walkway to a casino. An archway on the back wall of the hotel lobby opened to a large patio and garden. Parrots chained to their stands flanked each side of the arch.

He handed the desk clerk his passport.

The desk clerk opened the passport, scrutinized Connor's passport picture, then looked up and smiled. "Dr. Quinlan. We've been expecting you. Your room is ready."

Connor unlocked the door to his hotel room and walked into dead air at least ten degrees hotter and more humid than the lobby. He locked the door, threw his valise on the luggage rack, and switched on the overhead fan.

The room, slightly above the average Panama tourist accommodations, had light green walls, dark green carpet, muddy-brown and green striped drapes, and a gray bedspread with a pattern of bright green vines. Sliding glass doors furnished a view of the Pacific Ocean. Connor slid the patio door open, hoping the fresh air would lower the temperature in the room and clear the musty smell.

He stripped off his jacket and tie and tossed them on the bed. His shirt stuck to his back. Sweat dripped from his brow and stung his eyes. Connor swiped a handkerchief across his face, then spent the next ten minutes checking the room for surveillance devices.

The white porcelain tub and shower looked inviting.

He pulled off his clothes and hung them on separate hangers. *With any kind of luck, they'll dry in a day or two.*

He turned on the water—an anemic drizzle from the showerhead.

Ten minutes later, Connor grabbed a towel to dry his hair. The threadbare cloth was ineffective. He threw the towel on the bathroom vanity and swiped his hand across the stubble on his chin. His heart lurched. The reflection of a man's shadow reflected in the mirror.

"What-the..." Connor dropped to a defensive position. "Who..."

"It's just me, Connor. Take it easy." The man chuckled.

Ora sat in the chair next to Connor's bed.

"What's so funny? And, how the hell did you get in here?"

Ora continued to laugh. "You're funny, my naked friend. I came in through the door."

"I locked…" Connor stopped mid-sentence. Ora had the tools and the training to open almost any door.

Connor grabbed the towel he threw on the vanity and wrapped it around his waist. "They told me you wanted to see me. I expected a note or phone call, not an in-person, **unannounced** visit."

"I knew you were coming. I waited in the lounge and watched you check-in."

Connor took a deep breath willing his heart to stop the rapid tattoo. "What the hell are *you* doing in Panama? You're retired."

Ora gave an exaggerated shrug. "I got called back in to help with a problem. A little contract work with military intelligence every so often keeps my skills up to date."

The towel slipped. "Lemme get some clothes on."

Ora laughed, while Connor struggled to open his valise and hold on to the edges of the towel.

Connor nodded toward the doors to his balcony. "Did you notice the grassy area outside?"

"It would make a fine landing zone," Ora said.

"God knows we've evacuated on far worse. I don't think I'll need an emergency airlift this trip," Connor replied. He grabbed a handful of clothes and walked into the bathroom.

Connor stuck his head out the door. "I'm actually glad to see you. What're you doing here?"

"Same thing you'll be doing – gathering information. Donovan called me. He asked me to fly down here to meet with some of our old friends."

"Friends?"

Ora swept his hands, palm up in an all-encompassing gesture. "Friends from the School of the Americas. The Panamanians we trained at Ft. Bragg and Ft. Benning. Some of them are still our friends. They told me you were coming."

"How'd they know?"

"Word gets around when Mister Big Shot International Shipping Expert comes to town."

"What've you learned?"

"No one can tell the good guys from the bad guys. The only bad guy we know for sure is Noriega."

Connor nodded. "From the briefings I got, it doesn't sound like President Reagan is happy with the current situation."

"After the election, Noriega gave free rein to his Civil Crusade Organization."

"I'm well aware of that group of thugs."

Ora grimaced. "I heard they worked you over. How much damage did they do?"

Connor shrugged and rubbed his shoulder. "Could-a-been worse."

"Would-a-been, I hear. Good thing Jackson made one last sweep that night." Ora leveled an appraising glance at Connor. "You look okay to me."

Connor waved off Ora's remark. "What else?"

"Noriega's National Defense Forces are a bunch of thugs. They act as if they're loyal to him. After all, they do owe their paychecks to him. We're not sure how they'll react when they are tested." Ora rubbed his hands together. "Let's get down to business. I've talked to some of the National Defense Forces people."

"What're they saying?"

Ora gave an exaggerated shrug. "Right now, the Canal Zone is more American than Panamanian. Their army looks great on parade, but in a fight, they won't be worth a damn."

"Four weeks ago, our people at Howard Airbase were worried about what the reaction will be from the other Latinos. If we take out Noriega, they could use it as an excuse to set fire to Latin America. They think getting rid of the thug might excite the Russians and get our so-called allies upset. Hell, the Pentagon's even worried about how the Dominicans will react."

Ora shook his head. "So, they sent you here to test the waters?"

"No, I'm just a poor country-lawyer looking out for business. I have to meet with a few import-export people to talk about the time when Panama takes total control of the Canal."

"Shit, Captain, don't give me your poor country-lawyer crap. I figure you'll meet with the professionals. Be careful, Sir. I know the people the CIA sent me to meet. My contacts were guys we trained at Benning."

"Yeah. We trained Noriega at Benning as well." Connor waved off Ora's concern. "I'll be out of here in couple-a days."

Furrows appeared on Ora's forehead. "Don't trust anyone, Captain." He hunched his shoulders. "You don't want to end up dead. You came close enough to that on your last visit."

"The folks in Washington say it was a random attack."

"Hope they're right. If Noriega's flunkies have your number, they'll plant something on you to make you look crooked. Or, they'll kill you and make it look like somebody mugged you coming out of a cathouse."

Connor shrugged. "I'm told some of the businesspeople are concerned because their less scrupulous compatriots are selling out and dealing with the cartels."

No emotion showed on Ora's face. "Almost everyone in Panama seems to be making dirty money. My sources tell me some are afraid of refusing to deal with the cartels, while others are greedy, and all too willing to take the filthy money. We know where the dirty dealing begins, but we've not been able to trace where it ends. There's some speculation the money trail leads back to Washington."

"The less scrupulous people are dealing with the Colombians. They also have dealings with the Cubans." Connor curled his fingers into a fist.

Ora nodded. "Some Americans don't look too clean either, Sir. The rules in Panama have changed. I'm glad I'll be out of here in twenty-four hours."

A sudden picture of Anne invaded Connor's thoughts. "Will you have time to do me a favor when you get back to the States? I need you to make sure Anne's all right."

Ora's eyebrows went up. "Why wouldn't she be?"

"Just a feeling," Connor paused. "It's hard to explain." He tried to get his thoughts and emotions in sync. "I've always known when Anne's in danger. And, oddly enough, she knows when I'm in danger as well."

"How long have you been obsessing over Anne?"

Connor blushed. "Since we were little kids."

"Worrying about that woman almost destroyed our last mission."

Connor choked back momentary anger. "That's not the point. We successfully completed our last mission. So, are you going to help me or not?"

"Okay, okay, I'll check on Anne. Get over her. Women don't wait around for guys like us. They want someone who can take them dancing on Saturday nights, and take them out to dinner after church on Sunday. They want commitment – and kids."

"Damn it, Ora. Anne's in some kind of danger."

Ora held up his hands in surrender. "Don't worry. I'll make sure she's okay."

Anne
That Evening

Anne's long day was finally over. She rummaged through her briefcase.

Now, where in the world did I put my keys this time?

She searched her desk again. They were not in their usual place in the top left-hand drawer, nor were they under the papers.

No keys! With a soft sigh, she looked around the room. *How in heavens name did the keys get on the bookcase?* Anne scooped them up.

It's been a long week. I'm glad it's Friday. I need a few days at the cottage.

She shrugged on her jacket, picked up her briefcase, purse, and keys.

The architecture of the office building was unusual. Instead of a lobby, the hexagonal entryway held steps that descended on the left side to Thirty-first Street and another set on the right to Jefferson Street. Double glass doors lead to each of the three wings. Although guards patrolled the building at regular intervals, leaving in the gathering dusk was dangerous. It was not unusual to have the office exodus begin at about 3:30 p.m. on Friday.

I must be the last one out today.

Anne shut off all but the security lights and set the alarm for the weekend.

Because of the darkness, the glass doors were like mirrors.

Anne frowned at her reflection in the glass. *God, I look tired. A weekend at the Eastern Shore is just what I need.*

She glanced at her watch. *If I hurry, I can be in Newcomb before nine.*

Anne swung the door open and walked to the Thirty-first Street stairs. She strode up the hill toward her townhouse, invigorated by the breeze coming off the river.

At the townhouse, Anne checked the foyer and office.

Nothing felt strange or seemed out of place.

Relieved, she undressed as she climbed the stairs. She was anxious to get into some comfortable clothing. Her suit jacket and skirt went in the pile with her black dress.

Anne pulled on a pair of old jeans, a sports bra, her favorite green silk shirt, tennis shoes, and a sweatshirt. She retrieved a small duffel bag from the closet, packed a change of clothing, and picked up her purse before running down the two flights of stairs to the garage. The bag went into the back seat.

She ran back up to the kitchen and put some tomatoes, lettuce, celery, a lemon, and two oranges into a plastic grocery bag. She thought for a moment, then added a jar of capers, sliced olives, and a package of blue cheese. She slid a half package of English Muffins into the bag, picked up her briefcase, and ran back down to the car.

Anne looked at her watch while she waited for the automatic garage door to open.

Seven-ten. Not bad! Anne found her favorite oldies radio station and sang along as she drove across town.

Driving over the Chesapeake Bay Bridge, Anne felt the wind buffeting her car.

I wonder if there's a storm coming.

With time to think, Anne's thoughts returned to Connor.

She thought back to the years when they were growing up. Days of building sandcastles together when they were children, singing Christmas carols every year, then going to proms and family outings as they grew into adults. *He's my best friend.* She compared everyone she dated to him. No one came close.

Cards and letters from him during high school and college always had a drawing of a small island with a lone palm tree.

Since then, every so often, a postcard came with a pen sketch of their little island and its palm tree. Sometimes he added a stick figure sitting under the tree.

There were so many important things we didn't celebrate together. I missed all of Connor's graduations, and he wasn't at any of mine. He didn't help me celebrate the end of my residency, and I wasn't there when General Westmorland pinned a bronze star on his uniform.

Connor
That Evening

Connor checked his watch. Eight o'clock. Paola's limousine entered the hotel drive and stopped at the front entrance. Juan stepped out of the vehicle, stood at parade rest, his back against one of the hotel pillars, and waited. His dark eyes were covered with sunglasses.

Connor watched Juan. The man's head moved ever so slightly, side to side.

He's a trained security guard.

When Connor walked toward the hotel exit, Juan immediately opened the rear door of the limousine. Connor slid into the vehicle.

Juan secured the door, glanced over the area, walked around the vehicle, and slid behind the driver's seat. He slipped the car in gear and started toward the boulevard.

Paola adjusted the sleeves of her black silk evening suit, then leaned forward. "Please drive us to Señor Escobar's estate." She pushed the button to close the window between the front and back seats.

Connor waited while the window slid soundlessly into place. "Please, give me a rundown on the people I'll be meeting this evening."

"My employer, Eduardo Riesman, is the editor of 'La Prensa.'" She smoothed her skirt. "Eduardo's from a well-connected Panamanian family. He believes Panama should have authority over the Canal. He does not want any foreign government to have control of the Canal. It's Panama's most valuable asset."

Paola leaned toward Connor and lowered her voice. "La Prensa is the most influential newspaper in Panama." Paola paused, shook her head, and made a gesture of hopelessness. "Eduardo's solidly against Noriega… But if he published his true feelings…"

Connor nodded. He understood.

Paola took a deep breath. "An American named John Droges was invited to the dinner. The man is supposedly writing Noriega's biography. Mr. Droges is extremely vulnerable right now. In his opinion, President Endara is as corrupt as Noriega. He may be able to document a connection between Endara and Cuban drug dealers."

Paola paused again as if to gather her thoughts.

"Isobel and Roberto Duarte will be there. They are an interesting couple. Roberto's much older than Isobel and is the epitome of a smooth-talking Latin man. They run an import-export business. She's the stronger of the two. They have much knowledge regarding shipping, including the drug routes between Venezuela, Columbia, and Panama."

"Where are their loyalties?"

Paola gave a slight toss of her head. "They know how the drug trade is financed."

Connor made a face. "Not an uncommon stance in the business world."

"Manuel D'Ormondo will join us. He's upper management in one of our major banks. He told me he first met you at a meeting of the Panamanian Business Executives Association."

"Yes, I also saw him during my last visit to Panama. It's not a trip I'll soon forget." Connor rubbed his shoulder.

"Manuel comes from an old and very wealthy banking family. Much of his success comes from walking the fine line between ethical and unethical behavior. There are rumors that his family is profiting from the drug trade." Paola paused. "I have doubts. Manuel has an in-depth understanding of both U.S. and Panamanian culture, biases, banking, business, and government policy. His ties extend to Washington, New York, and Europe. He knows how the money flows. I doubt he favors Noriega, but he'd also be in jeopardy if he publicly opposed the man."

Connor knew D'Ormondo well and was aware of Manuel's hatred of Noriega. He smiled at Paola, "Our host?"

Paola laughed lightly. "Dr. Raul Escobar. He earned his Ph.D. in Economics from Harvard. He frequently jokes that degrees are a dime a dozen in Boston."

Connor nodded and smiled. "I've had the pleasure of meeting Dr. Escobar."

Juan pulled into a wide driveway and stopped before an ornate iron gate.

Connor could see a large modern home beyond the enclosure.

An eight-foot wall surrounded the grounds. Small guard houses stood at each side of the gate. Armed security guards stepped out of each enclosure and carefully checked their credentials. When the guards were satisfied, the gate opened.

Well-lit gardens fronted the three-story house. Juan stopped the vehicle near the base of a marble staircase.

A distinguished-looking man in his mid-sixties waited on the bottom step.

Raul Escobar pulled open the car door. "Doctor Quinlan, welcome to my home."

Escobar had a full head of gray hair and a neatly trimmed mustache. He wore a ruffled guayabera.

"Thank you for inviting me, Señor Escobar." Connor stepped out of the car and shook his host's hand.

Escobar waved Juan away and reached across the back seat to help Paola from the car. "Paola, I am so pleased you are here. You look beautiful. If you weren't married to a wonderful man, I would surely try to seduce you."

"And, you're as charming and flattering as ever, Raul."

He chuckled as he stepped between Connor and Paola. He escorted them up the stairs onto an expansive patio.

A manservant opened the door and ushered them into the villa.

Señor Escobar escorted Connor and Paola through an elegant foyer into a high-ceilinged room with white stucco walls and a parquet floor. Deep brown leather love seats and armchairs were arranged to encourage intimate conversation

Dinner guests, segregated into small groups, spoke in hushed tones.

Ornate candelabra flanked the fireplace. The largest mola Connor had ever seen hung on the wall opposite the fireplace. The native needlework depicted a colorful scene of a farm at the edge of the jungle. The handwork was exquisite. Felt cutwork animals, plants, and scenery pieced together and enhanced by decorative embroidery.

A large chandelier, anchored to the center of the ceiling, was made to work either by electricity or candlelight.

A silk Persian rug covered the central area of the room. The deep blues and rich burgundies complemented the furniture.

Despite its grand size, the room appeared comfortable and inviting.

"Doctor Quinlan, what can we get you to drink?" A servant immediately responded to Escobar's slight gesture.

"Martini, on the rocks with a twist, please," Connor answered.

"Typical American," Escobar chided. "You must try one of our rum drinks. You are not in New York. You're in Panama."

Connor gave a slight nod. "What do you suggest on such a hot night?"

Escobar murmured a request to the servant who returned with a tall rum punch. "It will quench your thirst far better than a martini. And, you won't look so American."

"What's the value today of not looking too American?" Connor inquired. "If I was a Panamanian, what would I hear that an American would not?"

Escobar laughed and put his arm around Connor's shoulder. "You want to know what we think? Become like one of us tonight. We are a complex and enigmatic society."

Connor asked in a low, quiet voice.

"Listen carefully. In Panama, you must choose your confidants with care."

Anne
The Same Evening

The wind pummeled Anne's car on the Bay Bridge. She clutched the steering wheel and didn't relax until she reached Kent Island.

Anne thought about Connor and their long-ago summers in Lavallette.

Building sandcastles on the beach when they were children. They hung out at Salty's Sweet Shop as young teens and sculpted sand mermaids. Their summer friendship eventually deepened to love. They were sweethearts. Parties at St. Benedict's Prep. Christmas carols sung at holiday parties. Dancing at high school proms. And their summers in Lavallette.

The empty spaces in their current relationship made her heart ache.

And, she remembered what he said the night before he left for Ft. Benning.

"Don't wait for me, Anne. I won't be back."

Connor
Panama
The Same Evening

"Friends," Eduard Riesman announced, "I would like to introduce our special guest for the evening, Dr. Connor Quinlan. A lawyer and expert in international port relations and shipping law."

Señor Escobar escorted Connor through the room with the smoothness of the most adept politician. Escobar exchanged news with each guest.

Isobel Duarte, a Latin beauty with dark eyes and luminous blue-black hair, disengaged herself from a small group, and sidled up to Connor. "Dr. Quinlan," she purred, "will you have a chance to relax and enjoy our hospitality?" She spoke English with a light Spanish lilt. "Why have you come to Panama?" Her gaze raked from his shoes to his dark curly hair.

Connor's system went on high alert. "I've been invited to consult with your government concerning the laws regarding maritime and international shipping."

"You are very knowledgeable in those areas." Her voice dropped to a low and throaty whisper. "I attended your lecture last year at the meeting of La Associacion Panamena De Executives de Empresa." She lowered her eyelids to half-mast and tilted her head. "I was **very** impressed." She took a deep breath and slowly exhaled. "I do not understand the intricacies of the legal issues. I hope you will find time to explain these subjects to me while you are here." Her tone did not suggest an interest in an impersonal conversation. "Perhaps we could meet somewhere for lunch?"

"I would be happy to answer any questions you might have."

She moved closer. "I know you would be a wonderful teacher," she whispered. "I am interested in international trade and have much to learn if I hope to compete with the men." Isobel reached out and stroked his arm and leaned forward. Her peasant blouse billowed out just enough to allow a glimpse of generous cleavage.

He straightened and smiled.

I'll need kid gloves and a chaperone.

Roberto joined them. "Dr. Quinlan," he said, "you must not be charmed too much by my wife. She is much too beautiful for me to leave alone. You Americans have taken much from Latin America already. I must protect my interests." he laughed and lifted his glass as if to toast Connor.

"Señor Duarte, I cannot challenge your statement. Your wife *is* quite beautiful. You are a lucky man. Any man would envy your good fortune." Connor pointed to his chest, "But, this is one Yankee who won't take her from you."

Roberto laughed and turned to his wife, "Isobel, beware of this American. He has the charm of a Latin, not the bluster of a North American. Are we sure he is a Yankee?"

"It's my Irish-American temperament and humor, Señor Duarte."

"Please, call me Roberto. May I call you Connor?"

"Of course."

"Perhaps before you return to the States, you will do me the honor of having lunch and exchanging thoughts."

Connor nodded and raised his eyebrows.

"We all need to share views during these troubled times. I would like to have your assessment on the future intentions of the United States Government."

"I'm just a legal counselor, Roberto. The United States government does not inform me regarding its intentions or plans. Even though I deal with international ports, I'm hardly the one they would consult about international relations."

"We will save our conversation for a later date." Duarte smiled as he turned to look over the room. "If you will excuse me, Connor. I must speak to our host."

Isobel leaned toward Connor. "Yes, we must also speak soon, Connor. Where are you staying? Somewhere quiet and safe, I hope."

"The Marriott." Connor averted his eyes from the display she presented. *These two operate as a very efficient team.*

Paola moved to Connor's side. "Isobel, do not monopolize Dr. Quinlan." Paola's words were soft, but the underlying warning was evident. "He must meet and speak to all the guests. You have charmed him long enough."

Paola led him across the room. Away from Isobel, toward Manuel D'Ormondo and Eduardo Riesman. The men were engaged in a serious conversation.

"Thank you," Connor whispered, "I felt like I was in the middle of a movie scene."

"Isobel is a most ambitious woman," Paola whispered. "I'm sure you have met others like her. She uses her wit, her charm, and whatever else is necessary to get what she wants. Her husband doesn't seem to care about her behavior. His permissiveness is unusual. Latin men are usually very jealous."

"I got the impression he approves of her behavior."

"There are rumors regarding his lack of prowess, and if I can put it discretely, his preferences. Some say Isobel has needs he can't meet. They seem to have a business partnership. Each is very ambitious."

"I've seen these kinds of couples before. Isobel behaves like the kind of woman we call a piranha."

Paola laughed softly. "Yes, I'm sure she could eat any man alive."

Riesman and D'Ormondo smiled at their approach. Riesman lifted his drink in greeting.

"Please join us, Dr. Quinlan. I was just telling Manuel he should find some time to talk with you. Manuel is very concerned about the future of Panama's international banking business."

D'Ormondo nodded, "I'm concerned about the financial instability in Panama. It would be good to have your perspective."

Connor gave a slight bow. "And, I was hoping to obtain information about the concerns of Panamanian businessmen and bankers. Some of my clients have interests tied to Panama's future."

"I have the advantage of my AP service and contacts with other journalists," Riesman added.

"What are the Americans saying about us?" Manuel asked. "CNN is my only source for United States business news." Manuel raised his glass. "We must talk."

Connor mirrored Manuel's gesture. "I'll drink to that."

Anne
Maryland's Eastern Shore
The Same Evening

Anne took a deep breath when she finally crossed the Oak Creek Bridge from Easton into Newcomb. Her dashboard clock read 8:37 p.m.

She signaled to make the turn to the short gravel road leading to her cottage.

I could use some company.

At the last second, she clicked off her turn signal and drove another three miles to St. Michaels.

I bet William and Stuart are having dinner at the Town Dock.

Anne scanned the patrons at the Town Dock. She recognized most of the diners and waved at several friends.

Stuart and William sat at their usual table. A waiter placed salad plates in front of her friends as she approached their table.

William looked up and smiled.

Stuart stood, "Anne, have you eaten?"

"Not yet. I worked late and left Georgetown as soon as I could."

Stuart pulled out a chair and gestured for her to sit. "We've just started our meal. Please, join us."

"I'd love to."

William signaled the waiter, "Chance, get Dr. Anne whatever she wants."

Anne scanned the menu. "I'll have my usual, Chance." She smiled at the young man. "A glass of Riesling, wedge salad, and a petit fillet."

A few minutes later, two men entered the restaurant. The maître d' pointed at tables near the far end of the restaurant. One of the men emphatically shook his head and pointed to a table close to Stuart and William.

The maître d' shook his head, and again gestured to the tables on the far side of the restaurant.

The taller of the two men pushed the head waiter aside and sat at the table near Anne and her friends.

Anne watched the exchange and wondered at the rudeness of the strangers.

"Hey – Anne," Stuart snapped his fingers to get her attention, "what have you been up to?"

She glanced at the men one more time.

"Anne?" Stuart broke her concentration. "How's work?"

"Same old same. I spend my days with young people coping with difficult situations."

"I can't imagine the stress of your job. I'd be suicidal after a week of that kind of responsibility."

"That's why you're a neurologist, and I'm a psychiatrist." She laughed. "But, I'm not always able to leave my patient's problems at work. My cure is a few days bathed in the peace of Swan Cove."

Their dinner conversation revolved around William's political aspirations and Stuart's position at Delmarva Health Plan. Anne half listened, and only smiled and nodded at what seemed to be appropriate times.

William nudged her. "Have you seen Connor recently?"

Anne smiled and nodded enthusiastically. "I had dinner with him last night."

"Last night?" William smiled, obviously pleased. "How is he? Why didn't he come out here for the weekend?"

"You know Connor!" Anne shrugged. "He's fine. He's off somewhere," she waved her hands, "doing whatever he does."

Connor
Later the Same Evening

Escobar's s servants opened a set of heavy mahogany doors. A waiter stood dead center in the opening and rang a small silver bell.

Escobar stood, placed Paola's hand in the crook of his arm, and led the group into the adjoining room.

The dining room walls were bright white stucco. Thick timber beams crossed the high ceiling. The parquet floor of the great room continued uninterrupted. Heavy Spanish Provincial furniture with dark leather seats created the illusion of a seventeenth-century Spanish estate.

A massive table stood on an enormous burgundy and blue Oriental carpet in the center of the room. The rug accommodated the long table and twelve chairs with a wide border to spare.

"My compliments, Raul." Connor's gesture encompasses the room. "This is as handsome a dining room as I've ever seen."

Escobar's smile and nod acknowledged Connor's compliment.

"Paola, please sit at the far end of the table and act as my hostess tonight." Escobar tipped his head to underline his request.

"Dr. Quinlan, I am honored by your visit. Please, sit to my right. Manuel, I'd like you on my left."

Isobel and Roberto Duarte walked around the table, checking the engraved place cards. A frown line creased Isobel's forehead. When she found her name, her look of concern turned into a coy smile. Roberto nodded. A smile danced across his face as well. He pulled out Isobel's chair and made a sweeping gesture for her to be seated, then slid into his seat at the far end of the table, left of Paola.

Paola smiled, then leaned forward to hear what Roberto was saying. She shrugged one shoulder as he spoke.

While Connor watched the interchange at the far end of the table, Isobel traced one finger along his outer thigh. "It's an honor to be seated next to you, Doctor Quinlan."

Escobar and Paola kept the table-talk light. No discussion of the problems facing Panama entered the conversation.

What seemed like an endless stream of Panamanian dishes were presented.

Connor especially enjoyed the entrée, seared tuna steak with a mango, peach, and cilantro salsa.

At the end of the meal, servers in formal dress swept into the room to present Tres Leches cake, coffee, and an assortment of liquors. The head waiter bowed to the group, then bowed to Escobar, and waited for the last of the wait staff to leave the room. He waited a few seconds before he exited the room.

Escobar watched the heavy doors close, then took a deep breath. He exhaled slowly and stretched his neck and shoulders and gestured to Connor. "I do not discuss issues while my staff remains in the room," Escobar whispered. "They are all good people. They've worked for my family for decades. But these are difficult times."

Connor nodded in agreement. "The underlying tension in the Canal Zone is palpable."

Escobar smiled and leaned back in his chair. "Many factions wish to turn the poorer classes against the business community."

"Several Latin-American countries are facing the same conflicts," Manuel murmured. "Panama is such a small country, and the Canal gives us an enormous amount of power. We've never had this kind of influence."

Escobar nodded. His voice returned to an average conversational level. "Are you familiar with El Chorrillo, Connor?"

"The impoverished section of Panama?"

"Yes. Many of my staff," Escobar gestured toward the closed doors, "live in El Chorrillo or have families who live there. Noriega was born and raised in El Chorrillo."

Connor played dumb and slightly lifted one shoulder.

Escobar continued. "Many of the Chorrilleros owe their continued existence to Noriega. They have no choice but to support him. The poor, the pimps, and the prostitutes are all lucrative sources of information for his henchmen. What's more, they are subject to horrible punishment if they openly oppose Noriega."

"We created the problem," Riesman interjected, "there has always been a huge gap between the classes. Panama never developed a strong middle class." He paused momentarily to sip his sherry. "Dr. Quinlan, do you know what the Rabiblancos are?"

Connor feigned ignorance. "My Spanish isn't good." He pulled his dessert plate back and took another bite. He savored the creamy richness, then added, "I know *Blanco* means white."

Riesman chuckled. "That part is correct. Historians tell us the phrase means 'White Tails.' No one knows the origin of the expression. It's what they've called Panama's elite for over a century. Most of the elite are white and are U. S. educated. They keep themselves as a class apart."

Isobel shook her head. "The class-war began a long time ago. Long before Noriega. The problem will never go away. Panama has two classes, the very rich and the very poor. There is nothing in-between."

"The Rabiblancos feel they have a hereditary right to rule," Manuel added. "They put a great emphasis on bloodlines. Their attitude has created a time bomb."

"Omar Torrijos exploited the class differences, and Noriega has taken advantage of the same theme," Señor Duarte agreed.

"A select few of the upper-class go along because Noriega makes it profitable for them," Escobar concluded.

"What do you think will happen?" Connor asked. "There seems to be much instability now. It was apparent on my last trip to Panama. I saw people brutally beaten in the streets. The threat to American military personnel is increasing. It seems as if La Dictadura has returned to Panama." He immediately realized he should not have allowed the term into the conversation. Connor coughed and feigned ignorance. "Wasn't that what they called the time Torrijos was the Dictator?"

"Yes, that's right," John Droges answered. "But Torrijos was only a de facto Dictator. He was the Commander of the Panamanian National Guard. It ended with his untimely and all too convenient death."

Several heads bobbed in agreement around the table.

"By the way, Dr. Quinlan, do you know Noriega was trained by the United States Military Intelligence?"

Connor feigned surprise.

Droges nodded. "It was the United States that turned Noriega into an evil person."

Connor knew Noriega's background. Connor had seen Noriega's file, including the notes from Noriega's instructors. Connor had been briefed, lectured, and re-briefed on every aspect of the dictator's career. He knew precisely how clever, calculating, and cunning the man could be.

The United States Government didn't make Noriega evil, Connor thought. *Noriega did that all on his own.*

Escobar stood. "We should return to the great room. We can relax with brandy and cigars."

Paola stood and accepted Escobar's arm as he guided the group back to the great room.

Servants appeared with trays of brandy and after-dinner cordials—a large box of cigars passed among the guests.

Escobar spoke quietly to Paola and gestured toward the concert grand piano at the far end of the room.

Paola nodded, walked to the piano, sat down, and began to play light classical music.

A servant approached Connor with a tray of brandy snifters. Connor chose one, then turned to examine the enormous mola, again. It was a fabulous example of traditional Panamanian fabric art.

Manuel D'Ormondo joined him. "You don't like cigars, Doctor Quinlan? They're the finest Cuba has to offer."

Connor shook his head. "A taste I never acquired, Señor."

Manuel gestured toward the mola. "Our native women produce beautiful artwork. Do you agree?"

Connor nodded. "I'm hoping to purchase several molas while I'm here. I'm afraid none of them will be as grand as this piece."

D'Ormondo lowered his voice. "It's good to see you again. I feared your previous adventure would be your last visit."

"The molas are a favorite of mine. I bought a few small ones during my last visit." Connor rolled the brandy snifter in his hands. "It's just by chance that I've lived to see you again," he whispered.

"It takes our native women quite a long time to produce a work like this." D'Ormondo lowered his voice, "If they knew who you were or what you were doing in Panama, they would have killed you. How is your arm?"

Connor restrained himself from rubbing his right shoulder." It only hurts when it rains or when I make love."

"Then I hope you have much dry weather but suffer much in love. How very Latin that will be." D'Ormondo gave a quiet laugh. "We must talk. Can we meet tomorrow evening?"

"Yes."

"On the French Plaza? A little after seven?"

"The Plaza? Are you sure?"

"My office and home are watched. I doubt anyone would recognize me in the Plaza."

Connor nodded. "I would appreciate your recommendations for purchasing this beautiful artwork." Connor moved toward the center of the room.

When the evening ended, Connor and Paola thanked Escobar for a wonderful dinner.

Still splendid in his guayabera, but now holding a large Cuban cigar, Escobar embraced Paola.

"When will Luis be returning to us?"

"It's still far too dangerous for him to return to Panama, Raul."

"May I speak to you for a moment? I have some information for Luis." He turned to Connor, "Please, excuse us."

Isobel Duarte reappeared. She leaned close and pressed her breast against Connor's arm. "I would like to spend some time with you during your visit," her voice was soft and sexy. "I am interested to know how trade through the Canal will change after the turnover." Isobel leaned forward, exposing her ample cleavage. "May I call you at your hotel?"

Connor felt the heat rise to his face.

"Just to make an appointment," she quickly added and widened her eyes. "Connor, you blush like a young boy. How wonderful."

Anne
The Same Evening

Anne said goodnight to her friends, ran to her car, and drove the three miles to Swan Cove. Rain, driven by gale-force wind, pelted her automobile.

Half the distance to her turn off, she glanced in her rear-view mirror. A car sped toward her, its headlights getting closer.

What does that guy think he's doing?

She considered moving to the right to let the car pass. A few seconds later, when she was sure he would smash into her car, she signaled the left turn into the lane leading to her cottage.

The car behind her fishtailed on the rain-soaked roadway.

Anne sat in her car to catch her breath. *I'm amazed he didn't hit me.* She took a deep breath, relieved the vehicle didn't crash into her Camry, gathered up her purse, then struggled to open the door against the wind. *I'll get the rest of the stuff in the morning.*

She fought the wind at the cottage door as well, entered the cottage, and latched the screen door.

Anne dropped her purse on the coffee table, grabbed a towel from the bathroom to blot the rain from her soaked jacket, then towel-dried her hair.

She knelt in front of the fireplace and stacked wood, kindling, and paper to start a fire. Thankfully, the dry wood caught on the first try.

The wind whistled through her large screened porch. Gusts created a hollow sound as it whipped around the large oak trees surrounding the cottage. The thump of branches knocking against one another added percussion to the cacophony.

Anne opened the back-porch door. A gust of wind caught the papers on her desk and sent them flying across the room. She struggled to get the door closed.

Her phone rang. She looked at her watch and frowned?

"Hello? Oh, Stuart – yes, of course I'm fine. It does look like we have a Nor'easter. I'll be fine here. I've started a fire. The cottage will warm up in no time at all. Thanks for worrying, I've ridden out a few of these storms, they don't frighten me. I'll be sure to call you first thing in the morning."

Stuart

Stuart hung up the phone. "Anne says she'd rather stay at the cottage this evening."

William shook his head. "Did you notice those men at the next table?"

"How could I miss them? They demanded to sit near us. What was that about? They each ordered one drink, but neither had dinner. They didn't even talk to one another."

"I think they were following Anne."

"The boss guy threw a fifty-dollar-bill on the table, and about broke his neck to get to the parking lot when she left."

"What do you think?"

"I'm not sure." Stuart shrugged. "Anne followed her usual Friday night routine. She drove out to the Eastern Shore to spend the weekend at the cottage. More often than not, she comes to the Town Dock for dinner."

"But her behavior may be new to them. I've never seen those guys in St. Michaels." Stuart scratched his head. "Have you?"

"No. They looked out of place."

"Anne said she had dinner with Connor last night. Do you think that could be the connection? Are they looking for Connor?"

"That's a possibility."

The men were silent for several minutes.

"She still has no idea we've known Connor for years." William laughed.

"I about lost my uppers the first time Anne walked through the door with him."

"I doubt Connor's told her he knew us years ago. I'm sure she doesn't know anything about his assignments in South America."

"And, she still has no idea we once had dealings with the Company."

"Let's get back to the point. What about those guys? Do you think Anne's in danger?"

"If I had to put money on it, I'd say they're looking for Connor." Stuart rubbed his forehead. "Sounds like he's out of the country. Anne told us Connor's on another assignment. I wish she'd agreed to stay with us tonight."

"Not much we can do about it now. I'll stop at Anne's in the morning."

Connor
The Same Evening

Connor settled into the soft leather upholstery of Paola's limo.

Paola asked Juan to drive to the Marriott Hotel, then pushed the button to close the privacy window. She turned to Connor, "Be careful with Isobel. Your description is accurate. She's a piranha."

Connor patted her hand. "Don't worry, Paola, I've dealt with her type before."

They arrived at the hotel a little after midnight.

"I'll call you in the morning," Paola said as Connor stepped out of the vehicle. "Get some rest. Tomorrow will be a busy day."

Connor wormed his way through the crowd on the hotel apron. He entered the lobby, turned to his right, and pretended to look at the goods displayed in the shops. His actual focus concentrated on the reflection in the store windows. It was an old but useful, technique to see if anyone was following him.

At the far end of the lobby, parrots perched on each side of the archway let out a loud squawk. Connor's attention was drawn to a cigarette flare from the darkness beyond the entrance to the back patio and formal garden. A man leaned against one of the marble columns watching him.

Coincidence?

Connor started up the staircase rather than using the elevator. *No CIA agent believes in coincidence.*

Anne
The Same Evening

Anne made a cup of tea, undressed, pulled on a t-shirt and cotton panties, then snuggled under the daybed quilt in front of the fire. Shadows and reflections from the trees blowing in the high wind danced on her windowpanes.

Raindrops pounded the windows and roof.

She sighed. *The last time Connor was here, we had a storm like this.*

They'd snuggled together inside the cottage. Their lovemaking had been warm and unhurried.

The thought made Anne smile.

It was the kind of night that made her believe her dreams could come true.

The reflected glow of the fire and happy memories erased her tension.

She gradually drifted off to sleep.

Connor

Connor walked up two flights of stairs, then stepped into the hotel elevator on the third floor and pushed the button for the tenth floor. He exited the elevator and walked to the eleventh floor. When the elevator doors opened, he rode back down to his level.

The temperature in his room was only a few degrees cooler than the hall.

Connor stripped off his guayabera and fiddled with the thermostat.

The sudden ring of the telephone startled him.

"Hello?"

A moment of silence. Then a whisper, "Connor, this is Isobel. Can you meet me for lunch tomorrow?"

He glanced at his watch. *It's almost one o'clock.*

"Tomorrow will be fine. I'll be glad to speak to you and Roberto. Where should we meet?"

"Roberto won't be joining us. I have no idea where Roberto will be tomorrow. We have our own lives. He didn't return to the villa with me. He has friends who amuse him."

Connor was stunned into silence. Because of their behavior toward one other earlier in the evening, her comments surprised him.

"I would like to have lunch with you tomorrow. We have much to talk about."

"I would be pleased to have lunch with you. Where..."

"I'll call in the morning." A click.

He wiped the sweat from his brow. *Isobel might be a fruitful source of information.*

Anne
The Same Night

A loud thump woke Anne. The storm raged. The wind screamed through the screened porch and howled around the corners of the house. Rain drummed on the roof.

Anne jumped out of bed and switched on the outside floodlights. Shadows danced across the yard. The wind whipped the tree branches. She stacked several logs on the embers, shivered, and once again snuggled under the down comforter.

About an hour later, Anne struggled in the gray zone between waking and sleeping.

Someone pounded on the door. "Anne, open this door." The pounding continued.

Anne fought off the last layers of sleep.

"Open this door right now."

Illumination from the security light flickered across the front room as the tree branches swayed and snapped. Flames jumped and flared as the wind gusted across the chimney.

The pounding became louder and more insistent.

Anne kicked off the down comforter, slid her feet into her slippers, and pulled on her robe. She searched the tabletop with one hand to retrieve her glasses. Then peeked through the curtain.

Herb stood on the stoop, his clothes soaked, and his hair plastered to his forehead.

She opened the door. "Herb?"

"Where is he?"

Herb jerked the screen door from its hinges and charged into the cottage. Rage contorted his face. He pushed Anne against the wall, stormed through the house, and yanked her closet door open.

She followed him the few steps to the bedroom.

Herb rummaged through the closet. Clothes fell to the floor. "Where is he?"

"What are you doing here? Who are you looking for?" Anne's emotions were a tumble of confusion, anger, and fear. "Get out of my house. There is no one here."

He turned, his face bright red, and shoved Anne out of his way. Herb yanked at the doors to the laundry closet. "Where the hell is he hiding?" Herb wrenched the bathroom door with such force the knob left an indentation in the drywall.

He flung open the French doors leading to the screened porch. Papers from Anne's writing desk flew through the room. He took a few steps left and right, then returned to the living room and mumbled incoherently.

Anne struggled to close the door. "Why are you here?" She turned to stand in front of Herb, arms crossed, back straight. "Who do you think you are?" Her anger bubbled over. "Get out of my house."

Herb grabbed Anne, lifted her off the ground and shook her. "Where is he?"

Anne purposefully let her body go limp.

Herb loosened his grip.

As soon as her feet touched the floor, Anne crouched, then lowered her right shoulder, and sprang, hitting his abdomen. Herb reeled back against her desk.

"I said – get out of my house." There was no mistaking the emphasis of her demand. "Get. Out. Now."

He furtively glanced around the small house.

"Did you hear me?" The timbre of her voice dropped dangerously low. "Get out now. I don't want you in my house."

Herb shook his head. He looked down at his soaked green jacket and the puddle he was leaving on the floor. "B-but...."

Anne walked to the front door and held it open. "**NOW**."

"B-but, Anne," he whined, "Annie…"

She slammed the door and stomped to the phone. Anne picked up the receiver and punched 'O.' When the operator responded, she said, "Operator, please get me the police." The set of her chin matched her anger.

Herb looked at her, opened his mouth, quickly shut it, opened the door, and sidled through the doorway.

As soon as he had both feet on the stoop, Anne dropped the phone, slammed the door, and set the deadbolt.

A muffled voice from the phone sent Anne scrambling for the receiver. "Yes, ma'am. I'm here. Thank you. I'm okay now. I was able to take care of the problem."

"This is Jeanie Horn. I'm the Talbot County Dispatcher. Who am I speaking to?"

"Oh, sorry, my name is Anne Damiano. I live in Newcomb, on Swan Cove. I had an intruder. I managed to get him outside."

"Have you locked the door?"

"Yes, ma'am."

"Do you know who he is?"

"Yes, ma'am. His name is Herb Smithfield."

"A friend?"

"No. He's someone from work. I've never invited him here. I have no idea how he found my cottage unless he followed me from Georgetown."

Anne watched Herb from the front room window. He stood in the pouring rain. He put one foot on the bottom step, then looked around as if trying to decide what to do next. Finally, he started to walk toward his car, then stopped again, and turned back toward the cottage.

Anne pressed the phone to her ear. "Yes, ma'am, he's no longer in the house, but, please, stay on the phone with me for a few more minutes. He's still standing outside my house."

Herb walked the short distance to his car, then turned to glance at the cottage, his shoulders slumped.

"Has he left your property?"

"Not yet. He just got into his vehicle. Thank you for staying on the phone with me, Ms. Horn. He just turned his left blinker on, but he's not moving."

Herb's car remained at the end of the lane several long moments.

Anne sighed with relief when she saw the taillights swing to the left. "He's headed toward Easton. Yes, ma'am, I'll be sure to call if he returns. No, I won't open the door. His car? A green jaguar."

She set the deadbolt on the porch door, mopped up the puddle on the hardwood floor, and propped the damaged laundry room door against its frame.

The Watchers
Newcomb, Maryland

The two men assigned to follow Anne watched the episode from the lawn behind the cottage. The French doors gave them a full view of the encounter.

"What the hell was *that* about?" Carlos muttered.

"Who knows? Wasn't Quinlan – That's all we care about."

"Should we report this?"

"Yeah, guess we better."

"We ought a go someplace to stay the night and get out of these wet clothes."

"The boss'll be upset if he has to replace us."

"He'll never know. Nothing's going to happen here until morning. She's not going anywhere in this storm."

Anne
Minutes Later

Anne felt violated. She stripped off her clothes, turned the shower on needle spray, and made the water as hot as she could tolerate. Her arms ached from Herb's grip.

The cottage felt defiled. There was not enough hot water or soap to dispel the chill or remove Anne's loathing of Herb.

How did he find this place?

The cottage phone number was unlisted. Everyone in Newcomb had a post office box. Postmistress Pattie would never give out an address.

The only markings for the turn into her driveway from Route 33 were two reflectors.

He must have followed me. But, when?

She shrugged into a terrycloth bathrobe and wrapped a towel around her hair.

Back in the front room, she added some crumpled newspaper to the smoldering fireplace logs and used bellows to reignite the flame.

She tried to visualize the lights in her rearview mirror during her drive out to the Eastern Shore. She shook her head. *There is no way to tell.* There were always cars headed to St. Michael's on Friday evening. She remembered the car driving so recklessly when she returned from the Town Dock. *Was he the crazy person who was speeding behind me when I left the Town Dock?*

Her stomach seemed to drop to her knees. *Has he been stalking me?* She glanced at the windows. The gauzy curtains would not have deterred a peeping-tom.

Connor
The Next Morning
April 18, 1989

The early morning sun streamed into Connor's room and reflected off the mirror on the far wall. He rose from the bed in one smooth motion and stretched. The sliding glass doors to the balcony provided a view of the ocean. On the distant horizon, he saw two ships heading for the entrance of the Panama Canal. The tide was out. Broad, dark brown mudflats, led to the edge of the water.

He pulled a small camera from his bag and snapped several pictures of the area.

The lukewarm, weak shower spray did nothing to ease the ever-present ache in his shoulder.

Twenty minutes later, Connor entered the dining room and breathed a sigh of relief. The hotel noise and confusion from the night before dissipated with the light of day.

Connor savored the flavor of the rich Panamanian coffee and ordered a light breakfast. *I wonder why the coffee in the states doesn't taste this good?*

He remembered Isobel's early morning call. *Is she bringing real information? Is this a setup or a seduction?*

Anne
Newcomb, Maryland

Anne grabbed her camera. This morning's sunrise was spectacular. She walked to the end of the dock. The swans that gave the Cove its name swam past her dock. They circled their fluffy brown cygnets and pushed them close enough for her to take pictures of their babies.

Anne laughed. *Proud parents are all alike.*

As she walked back up the slope to the house, she noted several limbs had fallen from the big oak trees.

William pulled into the yard. He waved. "Looks like you made it through the storm."

He stayed long enough to have a cup of coffee and stack the limbs in the side yard and promised to come during the week to cut the branches into firewood.

William pointed to the damaged screen door. "Looks like there might be a few more projects for me as well."

"They can wait." She gave a dismissive wave.

William looked at her with a question in his eyes.

Anne ignored the look. "There's always stuff needs fixing around here. Have they started the sailboat races yet this year?"

He nodded. "The first race is this afternoon."

"Great! Why don't you and Stuart come for wine and cheese at four-thirty? That's about the time they make the turn." Anne pointed at the red and white buoy in the channel fifty yards from her dock. It marked the half-way point of the race.

Felicia
Panama
That Evening

Felicia Alloto was born in Chorrillo, the poorest part of Panama City. She dreamed of the day she could live a secure life in a quiet, affluent suburb of the city.

Here in Chorrillo, the noise and the odors of the slum surrounded her.

Her family shouted and argued in the too-small house.

Neighbors screamed out the windows to their children.

Cars spewed fumes from poorly tuned engines. Radios blared.

The stench of garbage and human waste hung like a cloud over the entire slum.

Felicia gazed at her reflection in the cracked mirror. She knew her beauty and full figure were assets she could use to secure her future.

I need to get out of here while I am young and beautiful.

She turned in front of the mirror to admire her reflection. She had a flat stomach, full bust, and a firm rear.

Felicia lost her virginity at the age of thirteen. By seventeen, she knew how easily she could influence men.

She brushed her long black hair.

Tonight, she would meet Carlos, a neighborhood captain with contacts in the government. He led one of the Dignity Battalions, The local gang of thugs who terrorized the Chorrilleros.

Carlos is stupid. No young tough can take me where I want to go.

Felicia shuddered at the thought of his groping.

She looked in the mirror again and smoothed on her lipstick. *I need to get rid of Carlos and find an older, more established man.*

She readjusted her tight short skirt.

All men are alike. Get them hard, and they will do anything you want. An older man will give me security and social position.

She walked toward the old part of Panama City.

Carlos thinks any woman he screws is forever grateful. How stupid he is.

Her steps slowed and became more hesitant as she approached Plaza de Francia.

Felicia stopped walking. *Why should I give my favors to Carlos? Spending time with him isn't going to get what I want.*

Finally, she heaved a sigh and continued walking to the Café.

Carlos and Felicia listened to music for a few hours. He drained his glass several times. Finally, he threw a few pesos on the table and grabbed Felicia's arm. "It's time to go to the Plaza."

Plaza de Francia was built on a peninsula extending along the west shore of the Bay of Panama. The arches formed a circle around the plaza. Tablets carved into the walls commemorated the unsuccessful French attempt at constructing the Panama Canal. The Plaza was made as a monument to their failure. The mighty French nation brought down by the tiny mosquito.

Carlos pulled Felicia close and whispered in her ear. "I'm hot for you."

Felicia's steps slowed. She walked a few steps behind Carlos.

Carlos grabbed her arm and pulled her along. "Hurry. I want you **now**."

Felicia tried to shake off Carlos' hand. *He treats me like a whore.*

Carlos pushed Felicia against an arched alcove. She leaned against the brick ledge that faced the Plaza, spread her legs, and stuck her butt out.

Carlos struggled to push her skirt up to her waist then caressed her bare bottom.

She watched a man enter the Plaza. A last ray of sunlight illuminated his features. *Why would Manuel D'Ormondo be in the Plaza at this time of the day?*

Connor
Plaza de Francia

Connor scanned the plaza and the surrounding area. He noticed Felicia leaning on the ledge of the alcove. She seemed to be staring at Connor and Manuel.

A man stood behind the woman. He was bent forward, his hands on her shoulders.

Connor shrugged. *Must be a street-whore giving a john his money's worth.*

Manuel lit a cigar. The flare of the match pulled Connor's attention away from the archway.

Nodding toward the couple, Connor asked. "See the couple in the alcove? Do you recognize them? It looked like she's watching."

Manuel glanced at the archway and shook his head. His hand trembled.

Connor walked toward one of the arches and gestured for Manuel to follow him. *Manuel said only tourists, whores, and johns are in the Plaza at night. I hope he's right.*

Manuel reached into his jacket and pulled out a square white envelope. He handed the disc to Connor. Guard this with your life. Deliver it to the right people. The disc contains lists of accounts used to move money in the drug trade. Many banks are involved. Important people in the United States are involved, as well."

Connor slipped the disc into his shirt.

"They suspect me." Manuel made an abrupt turn and strode to an exit.

Felicia

Felicia waited.

Carlos was taking more time than usual. He grabbed her shoulders and rubbed his groin against her backside.

"Bend over…"

Felicia stuck her rear-end out a little further. *I think he's had too much to drink.*

Carlos was finally able to push inside her.

Bored, not moved in the least by his passion, Felicia continued to watch the activity in the Plaza.

Carlos grunted.

Felicia watched Manuel leave the Plaza. *Who did the grand high bank official meet?*

"Oh, Carlos," she feigned, "don't stop."

Carlos increased the feverish pace of his thrust.

Felicia wiggled.

Carlos grabbed her hips and groaned with relief.

Felicia reached one arm back to keep him tight against her.

"Stay inside me, Carlos. You are so big, so good!"

Felicia slung one foot around his ankle.

She continued to contract her pelvic muscles, knowing she could fool him.

Manuel D'Ormondo met someone in the plaza. Señor Reyes needs to know this information.

Stuart
The Same Evening

Stuart paced through his state-of-the-art kitchen. He grabbed a paper towel, dampened it, and swiped at a nonexistent stain on the oak countertop.

Stuart and William had just returned from watching the boat races at Anne's house.

"You told me there was some damage to Anne's cottage." He looked at Stuart accusingly. "You didn't say someone punched a hole in one of the walls, or that a door inside the cottage was damaged. And, I don't think it was the wind that pulled the safety latch and the hinges out of the door frame."

"You're right," William nodded. "Did you see the bruises on her arm?"

"Another thing you didn't bother to tell me about."

"She was wearing a sweatshirt this morning. We saw the bruises at the same time when she pushed up the sleeves on her blouse this afternoon."

"What do you think is going on?"

"I don't know." William stared at the countertop for a few seconds. "She's shared so much of her life with us over the years. Why wouldn't she let us know if she was in danger?"

"Do you think it had something to do with those two guys at the restaurant? It was obvious they were following her. They certainly weren't at the Town Dock for the ambiance, food, or drinks."

William frowned. "Stalkers?"

Stuart shook his head. "Stalkers act alone. They don't work in teams."

"She seemed a little distant Friday night. She wasn't her normal bubbly self."

The frown lines between Stuart's eyebrows deepened. Neither man spoke for a few minutes.

Stuart made a gesture of total exasperation. "Let's go over this piece by piece. We know the storm didn't cause the damage."

"And, the bruises on her arm look like fingerprints," William added. "What else?"

"She said she had dinner with Connor Thursday evening. Do you think something happened between them?"

William shook his head. "I can't believe Connor would ever hurt Anne. Besides, the bruises looked fresh. They weren't two-day-old injuries."

Another silence.

"Do you think it could have been one of those guys who came into the Town Dock?" Stuart rubbed his forehead.

"They looked tough. And, they did leave The Town Dock right after Anne did."

William shrugged. "Are we overreacting?"

"Do you believe in coincidence?"

"You've got a point." William's expression was grim. "I'll call Connor's office first thing Monday morning."

"If he's on another assignment, Angela won't be able to tell us anything."

"No, but she'll confirm that he's out of the office. And, there is the possibility she could get a message to him." William closed his eyes.

Stuart nodded. "Do you see any reason why we should call Donovan?"

"Don't even think about it. We're no longer associated with the CIA. There's nothing to indicate that Anne's damaged doors or the bruises on her arm are because of Connor."

Felicia
Later the Same Evening

Back in Chorrillos, Felicia remembered the lessons she learned in her first attempt to arrange a liaison that would get her out of the slum.

Marcos, a well-connected junior executive at one of Panama City's large banks, used his influence to get her a job at one of Panama's banks.

Felicia was bright and learned quickly. She enjoyed her work at the bank.

Marcos insisted on frequent sex. It was the expected payment for getting her a job at the bank.

I should have waited. Others could have helped me. But I wanted too much, too soon.

A self-degrading laugh burst from her. *I thought Marco loved me.*

Marcos was Latin handsome. Most of the young women in the bank found his athletic good looks attractive. He was one of the most eligible bachelors in the bank. As she heard the declarations of jealousy from the women she worked with, the more Felicia agreed to Marcos' demands.

I let the excitement of having what the others wanted to take control of my good sense. Why did I ever agree to meet him in the conference room that afternoon?

She believed Marcos when he said he would get her an apartment as soon as he got a better job. She trusted him when he said there was an opportunity in the personnel department.

Friday afternoons were usually quiet. Most of the senior executives were either relaxing after a lengthy lunch or already left for the weekend.

They met in the conference room, the blinds drawn to keep out the afternoon sun.

Marcos leaned back on the conference table. Felicia sat in a chair with head in Marco's lap.

One of the vice presidents entered the room to retrieve some papers.

She continued her activity until the lights snapped on.

That was the end of her job.

Marcos was from a wealthy family. His father was on the Board of Directors. He was just 'a young man sowing his wild oats.'

Felicia lost her job. She was labeled *puta—whore.*

Connor

When he got back to the hotel, Connor stuffed the disc D'Ormondo gave him in the middle of his business papers. He searched his travel kit for the small penknife.

He removed the bottom liner of his travel bag and carefully cut the seam on two sides of the fabric square. Using the knife, Connor traced the outline of the disc on the cardboard liner, then cut through the cardboard, and removed the circle. The bag now had a pocket just large enough to accommodate the disk. He smoothed the cloth cover and placed the bottom back in the bag.

Not great, with luck, it will be good enough.

Hot and sticky from the humidity, Connor decided to take a quick shower. *I hope it will help me get to sleep.*

When he walked back into the bedroom, the message light on his phone was blinking.

He had a brief mental flash of the woman watching the Plaza. A wave of cold fear wrapped around his gut. *Could she have reported my meeting with Manuel?*

Connor picked up the receiver and listened to the recorded message.

"Dr. Quinlan, this is Isobel Duarte. Please call me. I would like to join you for breakfast. I will be awake for several hours."

Connor remembered her suggestive behavior. He paused.

I can't ignore any possible source of information.

Connor dialed her number.

"Hello, Isobel. Yes, breakfast would be fine. Nine o'clock? 's perfect. A drink? Tonight? No, but thank you. I'm exhausted. The heat and humidity have taken a toll on my energy. Sleep well. See you in the morning."

Anne
Sunday Evening
April 19, 1989

Anne drove toward the bay bridge. Her mind jumped from one difficult patient to another, then finally to Herb.

Herb's become pathologically obsessive.

The Washington Social Circle considered him one of their most eligible bachelors.

Their last date had been more than a year ago. Since then, with every refusal, Herb's fixation on Anne became more intense.

Anne tried kind refusals, direct refusals, and avoidance. Nothing worked. Gentle attempts to ending their relationship only increased Herb's demands.

If she got a restraining order, the press would have a field day. She could see the headlines in her mind's eye. 'Herbert Jefferson Smithfield, Junior stalking a woman!'

Anne drove into the sunset. Layers of heavy clouds created ever-changing hues of gold, orange, and red as the sun sank lower on the horizon. The bay and estuary reflected the streaked sky.

She wished she could stop on the bridge and take pictures of the evolving scene.

Gloria Casale

Ora
Georgetown, DC
April 20, 1989

Ora stood in the shadows of the tree-lined street. He watched Anne leave her townhouse, lock the door, then walk toward Thirty-first Street.

The day dawned bright and clear. It held the promise of a sunny, crisp day in Georgetown.

Ora waited until Anne disappeared from sight, then lit a cigarette and smoked it down to the filter.

Just as he was ready to leave his secluded position, a tall man with auburn hair walked toward the townhouse. The stranger walked up the steps, pulled out a key, and unlocked the front door.

"I knew it," Ora muttered. "I told the Captain she wasn't waiting for him. She's livin' with some guy."

Ora stepped back and leaned against the tree. It was amazing how he could make his large frame fit into a shadow.

About forty minutes later, the man walked down the steps from the townhouse, got into a bottle-green Jaguar, and drove away.

Wait a minute. That Jaguar was parked on the street when I got here this morning. Ora shook his head. *He was waiting for Anne to leave. She doesn't know he has a key.*

The lock on Anne's front door posed no problem for Ora. He moved through the house quickly and silently.

Every room, decorated in soft colors and comfortable furniture, reflected warmth and comfort. Several small molas and pieces of Anne's needlework hung behind her desk. Filled bookcases covered the walls, and photographs in silver and brass frames were in abundance. He noted a black and white photo of a battle-ready, unsmiling Lieutenant Connor Quinlan standing in the yard of a fenced-off compound.

The second picture was Connor and Anne. It was a photograph from a high school prom.

Anne and the Captain have been friends for a long time.

There was no evidence of a live-in lover or even a frequent male visitor.

Ora slid the drape open a sliver. No one was walking in the neighborhood. The parked cars all looked empty. He slipped out of the front door, made sure the lock was secure, then strolled down Thirty-first Street to Anne's office.

He circled the building taking notes of possible unmonitored entrances and exits. There was one entrance from Thomas Jefferson Street, one from Thirty-first Street, and one from the underground parking garage. Several fire doors that were exit only.

The underground garage had a gate preventing unauthorized vehicles from entering, but anyone could walk down the ramp, skirt behind the gate monitor, and gain access to the elevator. The elevator did not require a code. However, the door at the top of the stairwell required a passkey.

Ora began to formulate a plan. He knew if he followed her for a few days he could discern her routine. Anne would shop in the same stores and talk to the same neighbors. If she went out for lunch or dinner, it would most often be to the same restaurants with the same friends. When he learned her basic patterns, it would be easy to keep her safe.

Anne

Anne hesitated before she pushed open the door to the institute. She dreaded another encounter with Herb.

Her secretary greeted her with a smile. "Here are your phone messages, Dr. Anne. "

"Thank you, Maggie."

"Um – Dr. Anne."

Anne looked up from the phone messages.

"Do you mind if I take an extra-long lunch today?"

"Problems? Anything I can do to help?"

"Oh, no. Nothing like that. Dr. Smithfield's not here. He took a sick day. Today's his secretary's birthday. So, the women in the office want to take her out to lunch. I'd like to join them."

"Of course, you can join them." Anne's tension slid away. "I hope you all have a great time."

Anne walked into her office.

Maggie knocked on the door. "l forgot to tell you – Sr. Empañada called – twice." Her tone conveyed disgust. "That man is rude. He wants you to call him back immediately."

"Thank you." Anne sank into her office chair and picked up the phone.

"Call me if you need anything." Maggie shut the door on her way out.

A man answered after the first ring. "Hola."

"Good Morning, Señor Empañada. This is Dr. Damiano. You called?"

"Helene continues to refuse to come home."

"Señor." Anne sighed. "We've discussed this so many times. Your daughter was brutally raped. The severity of both the physical and mental trauma she suffered was and still is, overwhelming."

"And, I've reassured both of you – the man who raped her will never bother her again. He will never bother anyone again."

Anne cringed.

"I warn you, Doctor, you **do not** want to make me unhappy."

Anne, clearly shaken, hung up the phone.

Fred Worthington
State Department
Harry S. Truman Building
Washington, DC

Fred Worthington sauntered into his State Department office, five hours late. He'd spent his morning on the golf course, followed by a two-martini lunch with his buddies. A note lay centered on his desk. 'I need to see you in my office as soon as you get in.' The Assistant Secretary of State's name was scrawled across the bottom of the note.

"Here we go again," Fred thought. *Another discussion from that jealous SOB about my work ethic.*

Fred strolled to the Assistant's office.

His secretary looked up and immediately pressed a button on her phone. "Mr. Worthington is here." She listened a moment and nodded her head. "Yes, Sir." She looked at Fred, "You can go in."

"Good afternoon, Mr. Worthington." The Assistant Secretary held an envelope marked TOP SECRET. A red and white striped border framed the edges.

Fred stared at the envelope.

"This came for you about one o'clock on Friday afternoon. Why weren't you here to accept it."

Fred felt his armpits dampen. His stomach started a slow roll. He met his foursome at the club for their usual Friday afternoon one o'clock tee-time.

"I had to leave early on Friday. A-um-doctor's appointment."

The Assistant Secretary checked his wristwatch. "Must-a-been a severe problem. Lasted until two o'clock this afternoon."

"Um – no, Sir – I had car trouble this morning."

"Did you get your vehicle fixed at the country club?" The man shook his head and shoved the envelope toward Fred. "Get out of my office. You need to start taking this job seriously. It looks like you may have something important to attend to."

Fred backed out of the room. When he reached his office, he slit the double envelopes open. The two-page memo from Killeen slid out.

Fred slumped into his chair. *This means trouble.* The clock on his desk showed two-thirty. *Killeen's going to be pissed.* Worthington shrugged. *Shaving a couple of strokes off my handicap was worth it.* He quickly scanned the information.

He chuckled as he read the memo. "Quinlan's in Panama, again."

He kicked his chair back and put his feet up on the desk. Fred's initial panic evaporated. This afternoon would be lucrative. Killeen's note put a double layer of icing on his cake.

Fredrick Worthington III was used to luxurious surroundings. His home in Chevy Chase was a showplace, furnished with beautiful antiques and expensive appointments. He was a member of the most exclusive country club. Fred demanded the best. And, used any means available to get everything he wanted. Seville Row tailors made his suits. His wife was dressed exclusively by Paris designers.

Fred remembered the advice his father gave him. "Remember, Freddy-boy, it only costs one third more to go first class."

Fred, the son of Frederick Worthington, Jr., was raised in Greenwich, Connecticut. His father was a prominent banker. Fred had graduated from Choate prep school. Because his father and grandfather attended Princeton, Fred's enrollment was guaranteed. It trumped his lackluster performance at Choate, and mediocre College Board scores. To Fred, Princeton was a series of parties punctuated with only enough classes to allow him to graduate. He didn't care enough to earn a gentleman's B.

He spoke fluent Spanish thanks to the time he spent at his family's vacation home in Costa Rica.

International banking was a natural fit for young Fred. It provided a bit of glamour and the chance of some international travel. Because of friends from school, and many family connections, Fred soon was assigned several lucrative accounts in Panama and Columbia. The banking system in Panama intrigued him. For the first time in his life, he showed enthusiasm learning the intricacies of the flow of money through South and Central American countries.

Unfortunately for Fred, life happened. The Carter years were terrible for the banking industry and disastrous to the Worthington family. Fred's father died suddenly, leaving his estate on the verge of bankruptcy. As word of the actual value of the Worthington estate became common knowledge, Fred's influential contacts disappeared.

Fred's friends canceled their accounts and refused phone calls.

Invitations to the Hamptons stopped.

Weekends on Fire Island became a thing of the past.

About the time Fred lost all hope, a friend from Princeton helped him secure a position at the State Department. It didn't take long for Fred to learn the income from government service was not adequate to support the style of living he demanded.

Other, less savory, contacts sought out Fred, offering him opportunities to increase his income. Fred jumped at every chance.

Felicia
April 20, 1989

Felicia arranged an appointment with Hector Reyes, the Dignity Battalion precinct captain.

She woke early on Monday morning to search her closet. Each article of clothing in her meager stash was carefully considered.

Felicia knew Reyes could offer her much more than Carlos. If he favored her, Reyes would make her life much more comfortable.

She chose a tight blouse with a deep scoop neck and a very tight skirt.

She scanned the underwear drawer, shook her head, and slammed it shut.

Señor Reyes must become as interested in me as he is impressed with my information.

Felicia looked at her reflection in the cracked mirror. She preened right and left, then tossed her hair, approving what she saw.

You'll be delighted with what I have to offer, mi Capitan.

Connor

Connor had finished his breakfast and signaled for the waiter a few seconds before Isobel entered the restaurant. "Buenos días, Isobel. You look lovely this morning." He stood and pulled out the chair next to him.

Isobel lowered her eyes and tilted her chin. "Gracias, Connor. Good Morning." Her clothing balanced the fine line between provocative and business smart. Her jewelry was expensive but not excessive.

When Connor resumed his seat, Isobel leaned forward. Her blouse appeared respectable when she stood. But when she leaned across the table, Connor had a full view of her cleavage.

The waiter poured a cup of coffee for Isobel and refreshed Connor's cup.

"We can't talk here," she whispered. "There are too many eyes and ears."

"The restaurant **is** crowded."

"And some of the patrons could cause trouble if they witness our conversation. I have important information for you. Come to my house for dinner tonight."

"Will Roberto be joining us?"

She shook her head. "Roberto will be gone for several days."

Connor weighed the invitation. Her hints of sexual favors disturbed him. But Paola's information indicated Isobel knew the intricacies of drug transport and money laundering.

"Give me your address." He reached to pull a pen from his jacket. "What time should I arrive?"

She reached out and stopped him from extracting the pen. "I'll send my driver for you at nine-thirty."

"Nine-thirty sounds fine."

"I must rush to my office.' Isobel took one sip of her coffee and stood abruptly. "I am looking forward to learning more about the legal intricacies of international shipping."

Hector Reyes

Hector was a robust man in his late forties. He was also a dangerous man who fought his way to the top with his fists and, on occasion, a knife.

Felicia entered his office.

Carlos Rodriguez's woman.

He curved his lips in what he hoped was a pleasant smile. *She insisted on talking directly to me.*

"You have information?"

Felicia turned sideways and ran her hands from her breasts to her thighs.

She's available for more than information.

Felicia watched him with hooded eyelids. "Si, mi Capitan. Carlos took me to La Plaza last evening. It was such a beautiful night. The breeze..."

"Yes, get on with it."

"I saw the banker, Manuel D'Ormondo, at La Plaza."

"How would you know D'Ormondo? You are a common Chorrilleros muchacha."

"I worked for his bank last year."

Hector Reyes shrugged. "So, he was there looking for a street whore. Half the bankers in Panama go to La Plaza for sexual liaisons. D'Ormondo's a rich man. He can afford high priced puta. Why would he go to La Plaza? Did you offer yourself to him?"

"I didn't approach him. And, he wasn't looking for a whore. He met a man."

Reyes laughed. "D'Ormando and a man? Is that what he likes? No wonder he goes to La Plaza."

Felicia shook her head. "No, he wasn't there looking for sex. I was surprised to see him in La Plaza, so I watched him carefully. He met a stranger and gave him an envelope."

"Tell me more about this encounter. What else did you observe?"

She shrugged. "D'Ormando was waiting close to the main entrance. As soon as the stranger approached, D'Ormondo handed him an envelope.

"I'm pleased to learn this. But, if you were in La Plaza with Carlos, why didn't he bring this information?"

"Carlos," she said with disdain and spat. "Il es un cerdo bourrache! He's drunk most of the time. And, does little with his battalion. Every night he's in the Café drinking pulque." She spat again. "He stays so drunk he isn't able to do anything well. He can't even please me."

"You were right to come to me. I will make sure you are well rewarded." Hector rubbed his groin.

"And, what is my reward, mi Capitan?" Felicia's hips moved in a suggestive circle. She pushed her breasts high to emphasize her cleavage. "Do you like what you see?"

"Yes, muchacha." Reyes moved from behind his desk, his erection evident. He grabbed Felicia's wrist and placed her hand on his groin. "This is what I have for you. I will make you sing with joy, muchacha."

Felicia sighed and smiled at him. She unzipped his trousers and slipped her hand inside. "I Como es grandees. How big you are. You are more of a man than Carlos."

Reyes put his hands on her shoulders and gently pushed her to her knees.

Fred Worthington
State Department

Fred Worthington held Donovan's memo. A frown creased his forehead.

If I send this message to my contacts in Panama, they'll know the US is plotting Noriega's fall. But they'll be happy to know Quinlan's in Panama.

Fred's private line rang.

"Buenos diás, Frederico." The voice was low and gravely.

The threatening tone sent a chill through Fred. "Ah, Buenos diás, Señor, I was about to call you."

Fred heard cynical laughter. His mouth went dry. A deep, dull ache under his breastbone made it impossible to take a deep breath.

"It's too late, mi amigo."

"Late? Late for what?" Fred stared at the notice, it was delivered three days before.

"My men followed Quinlan into the Metro several days ago. He outmaneuvered them. There's been no sign of him at his office or his home."

Perspiration coated Fred's face, head, and neck. His tailored shirt stuck to his back.

"Where is Quinlan, Freddy. You're paid to keep us informed."

"Quinlan's in Panama." Fred's speech was rapid, his voice almost a squeak. "I just received the memo today."

"What was the delay? You are assigned to the Panama operation. Perhaps your bosses know you are sharing information."

"No, no. The memo was delivered to my office on Friday. But I had to leave the office early. I had – I mean, my wife had a doctor's appointment. I had to drive her there."

"She was not the woman you were with at the country club. Is your wife's doctor's office attached to the golf course?"

Fred's stomach lurched. He realized they knew his every movement.

"What else does your Friday memo say?"

"Quinlan's in Panama. He's there to advise bankers and businesspeople. They asked him to provide information about ports and international shipping laws."

"Where is our friend staying?"
Fred could hardly breathe. "I don't know."
"Bastardo."
Fred heard a click. "Hello? Hello?"
The line was dead.

Connor

Connor entered the conference room of the Panamanian Container Line for an informal meeting. His role at the meeting was to shed some light on the future of the Canal Zone. The United States was to maintain joint control of the canal until 1999. In eleven years, the Panamanians would have total control of this essential link between the Atlantic and Pacific Oceans.

The businessmen knew the dishonesty of Panamanian politics. The center of today's discussion addressed tariffs and the future growth of trade. A variety of Chinese Companies were testing the markets in Panama and discussing future port operations.

Connor asked them to share their concerns regarding the joint management of the Canal.

Grave doubts about Noriega surfaced.

Everyone was concerned with his involvement in drug trafficking.

On the other hand, his assistance in obtaining the release of two American freighter crews from Havana was a point in his favor.

And, they discussed the fact that he laundered drug money and the rumors they'd heard about his sale of restricted American technology.

When the meeting adjourned, white-clad servers rolled two large carts into the room. The businessmen helped themselves to drinks and tasty entremets from sumptuously laden trays.

"A drink, Dr. Quinlan? Something to fortify you until dinner?" The meeting moderator gestured toward the open bar.

"Yes, thank you." Connor leaned against the wall and listened to the conversations swirling around him.

The discussion topics centered on issues of Canal economics. Eventually, the conversation turned to politics. The guests expressed much bitterness and dissatisfaction with Noriega's regime. They hated and feared Noriega and his use of power to diminish their influence and wealth. Much of the discussion centered on the Dignity Battalion's brutality and extortion. The businessmen worried about violence.

Noriega's thugs were given free rein.

"What do you think about the pirate radio?" someone asked.

Connor stood aside to listen and sip his drink.

Manuel sidled up to him. "I've heard Noriega's furious. He's doing everything in his power to find the guy who runs that station."

They're talking about Kurt. Connor took another sip of his drink and concentrated on the conversation.

Isobel nodded. "The broadcasts are clever. Popular music with periodic short messages against Noriega."

"I think he must move frequently. If the transmitter stayed in one place, they'd have caught him by now."

"I wouldn't want to be in his shoes when they find him."

"What do you think they would do to him?"

Connor didn't engage in the swirl of comments.

"Modella prison and torture."

A gloomy silence pervaded the room.

Connor squared his shoulders to rid the uncomfortable feeling of spiders crawling over his body. Scenes from his time in Special Forces ran like a movie in his mind. He was aware of what 'the end could be for Kurt.'

Finally, Emanuel spoke. "The Dignity Battalions control the residents of the Chorrillo by fear. Most of the Chorrilleros swore allegiance to Noriega. He said he would raise them out of poverty. Now, because of the power of the street toughs, they can only continue to profess undying loyalty to him. Some are starting to realize he's not their savior. People are afraid. One word against Noriega or any of the Captains ..." He shook his head.

"He'll only give them more poverty and more pain."

"Noriega doesn't want information broadcast by anyone."

"Who's operating the radio?"

"Either a brave man or a foolish one."

"I'm willing to bet he isn't a Panamanian."

"I wonder if the station is off-shore."

"I'd guess he's an American. Maybe CIA."

"I'm sure his broadcasting days are numbered."

"Someone is bound to provide Noriega with the man's identity. Whoever identifies the person will gain great favor and reward from El Presidente."

Anne
Georgetown, DC

On her way home from the office, Anne stopped at **'YES!'** The bookstore carried an eclectic variety of books and music. A chime announced her arrival.

The woman behind the desk looked up. "Dr. Damiano," the clerk's broad smile welcomed Anne. "Great day today, don't you think?"

"Hi, Jani. It has been a nice day. It looks like spring is finally here."

A pleasant smell of incense permeated the store.

Anne found a book on the history of women in medicine.

"Good choice, Dr. Anne," Jani Krebs rang up the purchase. "What do you have planned for this evening?"

"I'm hoping to have dinner at La Ruche. Since it's so early, I should be able to get a table without the usual wait. Then, with any luck, I'll go home, put my feet up, and relax."

Jani smiled. "Sounds like a great plan." The clerk pulled a bag from under the counter.

"I don't need a bag. I'll just slip the book in my briefcase."

An hour later, Anne left the restaurant. She looked at the gathering dusk and made an impulsive decision to say a quick prayer at Christ Church. An ancient oak tree stood beside Christ Church. The Church elders regarded the tree as their symbol of strength and peace.

Anne crossed her fingers, hoping the chapel was open. She walked down the alley to the stone steps.

To Anne's surprise and delight, the chapel was open. She slipped through the door and knelt in one of the back pews. The darkened nave provided a welcome haven, allowing the solitude to fill her mind and heart.

Herb
Georgetown

Herb lurked outside the bookstore, followed Anne, and now waited at the edge of the churchyard.

He peeked around the corner of the building, watched Anne leave the church, and considered his next move.

Herb straightened his jacket, then pushed his shoulders back and took a few steps toward Anne. *I'll catch up to her and force her to listen.*

He nodded. "I'll make sure she understands."

Anne was halfway up the street.

Herb started to sprint after her.

Someone grabbed him. The attacker spun Herb around and slammed him against the oak tree, pressed his face against the rough bark, and locked his arm.

A gravelly voice with an indefinable accent whispered, "Stay away from the lady."

Herb felt a slight pressure on his neck, then felt nothing at all.

He woke with soiled pants, afraid to move. When he was sure he was alone, Herb checked his pockets. His wallet, watch, and keys were still there.

Connor

Connor glanced at the clock over the registration desk in the hotel lobby. *Nine-thirty.*

Isobel's driver snapped to attention when the clerk gestured toward Connor.

The Duarte house sat on a hill overlooking the city. Elegant, well-tended gardens flanked both sides of the walled courtyard surrounding the entrance. A manservant ushered him into the foyer. Isobel moved slowly down a set of curved stairs to the foyer. Her full-length filmy dress flowed as she walked toward him.

Connor watched the sheer material settle seductively over her curves. "Connor, thank you so much for agreeing to have dinner with me."

Isobel extended her hand, palm down toward Connor. Much like a princess seeking subservient esteem from an admirer.

Connor took her extended hand and inclined his head. "It's my pleasure, Isobel. I don't often get invited to dine with such a beautiful and charming woman."

She ushered him into a high-ceilinged sitting room with subdued lighting, and deep comfortable chairs, and quiet background music.

A glass-paned door separated the sitting room from a small dining room.

Isobel took Connor's arm and gently guided him into the dining room. She spoke to her butler in rapid Spanish. Within minutes, he served Connor a sweet, refreshing, strong rum drink.

Isobel gestured toward a table set for two, its centerpiece flanked by flickering candles. The candles provided the only light in the room.

Isobel's house-staff was efficient. And, her skills as a hostess honed to perfection.

She kept their dinner conversation light, amusing, and non-substantive. She talked about international trade from Central America. The remainder of the dinner conversation included humorous incidents that occurred between Panamanian businessmen and shipping companies.

Connor wondered if she would ever get to the point.

"We'll have coffee in the library," she said as if she could read Connor's mind.

Connor and Isobel entered the library through an elaborately carved door.

The library walls were covered with highly polished wood paneling. Full-length bookcases filled with leather-bound books flanked the doorway and the sidewalls. Two large and colorful molas hung on each side of the stone fireplace on the opposing wall. The room had no windows. The single door was the only exit.

I bet this room seals off with the touch of a button.

Two deep, soft leather sofas faced each other in the center of the room. An elaborately carved table stood between them.

Isobel gestured toward the arrangement. "Please sit down, relax."

Soft music filtered into the room, an additional buffer to ensure privacy.

The coffee service and tray were heavy silver, etched and engraved with a family crest.

Isobel poured coffee into china cups. "Sugar? Cream?"

Connor shook his head. "No point in ruining the flavor of Panamanian coffee. I'll take it black."

The tray also held a bottle of Averna Sambuca and two glasses. Three coffee beans rested in each glass.

Isobel expertly poured the Sambuca, then lit the strong anise-flavored liquor.

Connor smiled and nodded. He swirled the liquor to snuff out the flame, then lifted his glass.

"I have information regarding the current trade between my native Columbia and your country." Her voice dropped lower, enticing him to move closer. "It's ugly. I've discussed the situation with Paola. She suggested I talk to you."

Connor breathed easier.

"Several trading companies ship drugs in containers from Columbia to Panama," Isobel whispered. "They've attempted to induce some of my workers to place their goods inside my shipments. My men have been offered bribes. So far, we've been able to refuse to accept their shipments." She paused, then continued.

"We know the Cartel will kill anyone who succeeds in stopping them. Roberto is frightened. He wants to give up the business and leave the country. I'm frightened too, but I don't want to run from these animals." She tossed her head. "I'm more of a man than he is. One needs balls in our business."

She suddenly stopped and put her hand over her mouth. A tentative smile, and a wave of her hand. "I'm just a woman in a man's world of business."

Isobel ran her hands along her bodice. "A few honest businesspeople in Panama are attempting to stop the cartels from taking over. But people in our government, as well as in your government, are working against us."

She stood, walked to a bookshelf, and opened a cabinet hidden behind fake books. Isobel's dress shimmered as she pulled out a sheaf of papers and carried them to Connor.

"Read these carefully. The documents **cannot** leave this room." She turned, allowing the yellow silk to swirl around her hips and legs. "Please excuse me for a few minutes."

Connor looked over the papers. Lists of companies in the United States and their trading partners in Columbia. Notations of each company's connections to the drug trade. And information regarding the names of American businesspeople who are involved.

He realized the list of documents and descriptions could be accessed in the United States. The technicians in the United States would need this data to corroborate the evidence.

Isobel returned about ten minutes later and smiled. "I hope you had enough time to digest the information." She reached for the documents. "By the way, Roberto sends his greetings."

Isobel straightened the papers, slid them in the alcove, and shut the door.

Connor heard the muted sound of a lock shifting into place.

"The men identified in those records would not have qualms about eliminating anyone who knows their names and connections. The documents will remain here. They would kill you if they found them on you or in your hotel room. If the Cartel, or anyone in the Panamanian or Columbian governments, could trace them back to me, I would disappear and never be seen or heard from again."

Prickles played across Connor's neck. He was wary about uncorroborated information. He drummed his fingers on the arm of the couch.

The entire evening was beginning to feel like a scene in a poorly written spy movie.

Connor's mind whirled with possibilities. *Is this a setup?*

He took a deep breath. "I'm not sure if I can do anything to help you, Isobel. But I'll try to find people who can."

She arched her eyebrows. "I am sure you are more than just an attorney with expertise in port transport."

Connor gave a dismissive shrug. "I will remember the details of the trade. But I'm not sure if I would be able to find anyone who would listen."

Isobel sat on the sofa, placed her elbow on her knee, and rested her chin in her hand. "I'm sure you can help us."

"All I can do is try to find someone in Washington who cares. If I find them, they will demand corroborative evidence."

"I have information on dates and places. I can't provide the names of the people in your government who turn a blind eye or accept payment for assisting the cartels. But I know the names of banks and companies laundering the money. The Columbians left records on our computers. Their dealings appear legitimate unless you know what to look for."

She waited a few moments then shifted uneasily when Connor didn't respond. "When I am sure no one will come after me, I'll provide even more information." Isobel leaned toward him and whispered, "Do not treat this information lightly. If you aren't what I hoped, I'll be in great danger. You now have information that could cost me my life."

Connor realized both Isobel and Manuel D'Ormondo gave him a roadmap to the money trail.

He suspected it would lead to American officials.

And, he realized he'd misjudged her and marveled at her courage.

"I will not betray your trust, Isobel."

She lifted her drink. "A toast to a trusting relationship."

Minutes later, Isobel placed her drink on the coffee table, leaned toward him, and kissed him.

Connor tasted the sweetness of her lips. He felt her tongue encouraging him to open his mouth.

He gently moved away from Isobel and sat back against the leather sofa.

"Permsenzia por favor un rato. Please stay at least for a while. Stay with me tonight."

"No, Isobel. But thank you for the invitation."

Isobel waved her hand. "Perhaps another time, then. The invitation will remain open."

Connor stood to leave. "It's late, and I have a busy day tomorrow."

She moved close to Connor. "Stay the night... I need a man. Roberto will not be back until tomorrow."

Connor put his hands on her shoulders and took a step back. "Isobel, your safety is paramount. Foolish flirtation won't help either of us."

"Another time and place perhaps."

Ora
Georgetown
April 21, 1989

The next morning, Ora waited in the niche between buildings across from Anne's townhouse. He watched her pull the heavy oak door closed, cinch the belt on her trench coat, and run down the steps. She turned and walked toward Thirty-first street.

Ora stepped away from the building and leaned against a tree until he saw Anne turn the corner and start down the hill toward the Institute. It was the same route she walked yesterday.

Half a block away, a man stepped from a parked car, quietly closed the passenger door, and strode toward Anne. When he started down the hill, he was about fifty feet behind her.

Now what? He's not the green Jaguar guy.

Ora strolled down the street. He varied his pace, stopped briefly to tie his shoe, and paused again to light a cigarette.

When Anne stopped for traffic, the dark-haired man following her waited. He never closed the distance between them.

At the entrance to the Institute, Anne set her shoulders, climbed the concrete steps, and entered the building.

The strange man stopped for a moment, shook his head, and continued walking toward Washington Harbor.

Ora hesitated, torn between following the man and canvassing the Institute. He decided to check out the institute. Ora waited for a break in the foot traffic, then entered the lobby.

Four elevators flanked by full length mirrored windows, stretched the length of the south wall. The entrance from Thirty-first Street was on the east side of the lobby, and a door to Thomas Jefferson Street was on the west side. A staircase led to the upper floors, but also down to what Ora presumed was the parking garage. Double glass doors on each side of the stairs opened to reception areas.

Ora walked down the steps. The single-level parking garage appeared to have the same dimensions as the building proper. A single entrance from Thirty-first Street had an electronic gate and a punch code meter. The gate only controlled for vehicles. Anyone could duck under the metal arm and gain access to the parking garage and the elevator.

There were no security locks. Anyone could enter the lobby from the staircase or the elevator. Ora returned to the lobby and entered the hall leading to the reception desk nearest the Jefferson Street entrance.

"Good Morning, sir, how can I help you?"

"I'd like to leave a message for Mr. Bernowski."

"There's no one by that name in the Institute."

"Oh?" Ora pretended surprise. "I'll check across the hall. Perhaps his office is in the other wing."

The receptionist shook her head. "No, sir, there is no one at the institute named Bernowski."

"I'm sorry," Ora shrugged his shoulders. "Perhaps I have the wrong address."

He left the reception area and walked up the stairs.

Every level had entryways to the wings. Entry keypads protected each level.

Anne
The Institute

"Good Morning, Cindy." Anne smiled at the receptionist.

"Good Morning, Dr. Damiano. You look like a ray of sunshine despite the gloomy day."

"Thank you."

Anne continued down the hall, unlocked her office door, hung up her coat, and opened her appointment book.

She dialed zero. "Cindy, hi, again, please screen my calls. Thanks. I appreciate it."

Anne dialed an outside line. "Hi, Stuart. I'm thinking of driving over to the cottage this afternoon and having dinner at the Town Dock. Would you-all like to meet me there at about eight o'clock? Great. Can you make the reservations?"

Herb pulled open the door to Anne's office and stormed in.

She gasped. Herb's face was bruised and scraped. "What happened to your face?"

"I'm sure you've already heard all about what happened."

"What are you talking about?"

Herb leaned across her desk. "Don't play dumb with me. Your goon can't scare me."

"My what?"

"Make sure it doesn't happen again. If that guy even comes close to me, I'll shoot him."

"Get out of my office **now**."

Herb wheeled around and stalked out the door.

My goon? Anne took a deep breath and stared at the picture of Swan Cove.

Moments later, she dialed Maggie. "Please cancel all my appointments for the day." She paused a millisecond. "On second thought, cancel all my patients for the rest of the week. And, please, put me through to Director Frye."

"Anything else?" Maggie inquired.

"No, thank you. I hope you have a good week."

Anne cleared her decision to take the week off with the Director. While she was there, she expressed her concerns about Herb.

The Director reminded Anne about the support Herb's family donated to the institute.

Anne stood and locked her desk. She shrugged on her trench coat and secured her office door.

Ora
Georgetown

Anne almost collided with Ora when she stormed out of the Institute. He turned and checked his watch, then followed her back to the townhouse. No one else joined her daily cadre of followers.

Later in the afternoon her Camry backed out of the garage. Anne headed East.

Ora followed her over the Bay Bridge to the Eastern Shore. She drove directly to the Town Dock. Ora waited a few moments before he got out of his car and entered the bar.

The bartender nodded to him and pushed a dish of pretzels and peanuts toward him. "What can I get you to drink, sir?"

"Whatever beer you have on tap, please."

Ora's seat at the bar allowed him a view of Swan Cove and the boats docked at the restaurant's deck, as well as keep an eye on Anne. She half reclined on a lounge chair, sipping a Bloody Mary.

The weather had cleared. The sunset over the inlet to Swan Cove was spectacular.

"Here you are, sir," the bartender smiled. "Will you be having dinner with us?"

"Haven't decided yet."

The bartender wiped non-existent spots from the highly polished wood. She smiled again. "Are you new to the area or just visiting?"

"Just passing through. Thought I'd see what the Chesapeake Bay has to offer. I'm in Washington on business and was able to take a little time off."

The bartender nodded, then moved off to take another order. She was not only pleasant and efficient, but also attractive. Ora's eyes followed her. When his gaze returned to the dock, he noticed two new customers now sat at a table close to Anne.

Anne was scrunched down. Her face turned toward the setting sun.

There isn't much coincidence in the entire world, Ora thought. *That's the same guy who followed Anne down Jefferson Street this morning.*

Ora moved to a stool at the end of the bar to get a better view of Anne.

A little later, William and Stuart entered the restaurant. Customers waived and called to them.

Ora's glance slid to the right. He all but choked on his drink. *Stuart and William? Is that what they call themselves now?* He quickly averted his eyes and lowered his head. He shielded his face with his right hand.

Ora hadn't seen the men in several years. The last time he saw them was in Bogota at the safe house they operated.

"Hi, Rosie," the one that called himself Stuart said to the bartender. "We'll be out on the deck with Dr. Anne. Please have Chance bring a beer for William and my usual sake Martini to her table."

"You got it, Stuart. They'll be out there real quick."

Ora was stymied. *And, they're going to sit with Anne. How do they know her?*

Each man hugged Anne. She smiled and returned their embraces.

Does Anne know who Stuart and William are? Or at least who they were?

Rosie interrupted his musing. "Hey stranger, you look like you're carrying the weight of the world on your shoulders. Can I refill your drink?" She pointed to his empty glass.

"Yes, please, Rosie. And I've decided to stay for dinner. Any suggestions?"

Anne

Anne gave Stuart and William a weary smile. "I'm so glad you all could meet me for dinner." Her voice sounded tired.

"What's the matter?" Stuart frowned. "Must be something serious for you to drive out here on a weeknight."

"It *is* serious. I'm taking the whole week off. I have a lot to sort out, and I need help to do it."

Both Stuart and William looked at her wide-eyed, their mouths dropped open.

"The damage to the house last weekend wasn't from the storm." She paused and took a deep breath, "I dated one of the men I work with last year. We only went out a few times. He showed up at the cottage Friday night – during the storm. It must have been close to midnight. He knew I had a cottage somewhere on the Eastern Shore, but I never mentioned Swan Cove or Newcomb. He must have followed me out here on Friday night. I never told him anything about St. Michaels. I never…" Anne stopped short when she realized she was babbling.

William patted her arm. "Slow down and tell us what happened. Take it one step at a time."

"Okay, I'll try." She massaged her forehead and collected her thoughts. "After I left the Town Dock on Friday night, I went back to the cottage, started a fire in the fireplace, and fell asleep on the day bed. I woke up because I heard pounding on the door." She shivered. When I opened the cottage door, Herb ripped the screen door off its hinges and charged in the house." She choked and started coughing.

"Take a deep breath, Anne." Stuart's voice was soft. "We have all the time in the world."

She nodded, took another deep breath, and exhaled slowly. "Herb stomped through the rooms shouting, 'Where is he?'"

William held her hand. "Who was this Herb person looking for?"

"I don't know. Herb just kept shouting, 'Where is he?'"

"Where was who?"

Anne shook her head. "I don't know."

"What about the bruises on your arms?" Stuart stroked her right arm.

"Herb grabbed me, lifted me off the floor, and shook me." Anne's face flushed.

"My God," the men breathed in unison.

"I remembered the class I took on how to foil an attacker training and went limp. It works. He let go."

"Then what?" The deep line in Stuart's forehead was more pronounced.

"I scrambled for the telephone and asked the operator to connect me to the police."

"Did he leave?"

"Yes." Anne's vigorous nod and sigh underlined the relief she felt. "The dispatcher stayed on the phone until I told her Herb pulled onto the highway. She asked which direction he went and what kind of car he was driving."

"Why didn't you call us?"

"It was the middle of the night. I cleaned up the puddles from Herb's dripping clothes and straightened the cottage as well as I could. Then I took a shower. I guess I was trying to wash off even the memory of his touch."

"Was that the end of it?"

"No, Officer Clyne came to the cottage and took a report. He said the Easton police detained Herb."

"Have you seen this Herb person again?"

"I don't have a choice. We work in the same building in the same department. This morning Herb stormed into my office and started ranting about being attacked. He had abrasions on his face and insisted I'd hired someone to beat him up. Said he was going to shoot the guy."

"I'm sure you didn't hire anyone."

"Of course not – I don't even know where to start doing something like that."

"Does he have a weapon?"

"He said he had a gun."

"Anne, you need to report this incident to the Georgetown police and have them contact Officer Clyne for a report on the episode at your cottage."

"I reported his behavior to the head of the Institute. And, I don't need all the publicity an official police report would engender."

"But, Anne -"

"I'd lose my job."

"Because someone attacked you?"

Anne spread her hands in a gesture of helplessness. "Herb's family is part of the social elite of DC. They contribute huge amounts of money to the Institute. They've got power and pull. I'd get fired."

Connor

Connor walked down the hall to his hotel room and heaved a sigh. *I'm glad this round of meetings is over. I need an evening of relaxation.*

Connor stopped short. The small matchstick he placed in the door was lying on the floor. *Someone's been in my room.*

He wiggled the handle, then put his key in the lock and turned it. No sounds came from inside the room.

Connor stepped to the hinge side of the door, put his back against the wall, and carefully turned the handle, then pushed the door as hard as he could. The solid wood hit the wall with a resounding crack.

The room was in disarray. Connor's travel bag was upside down on the floor. Dresser drawers open, their contents were strewn across the bed. His shaving kit emptied into the sink.

He checked under the bed, the bathroom, and the balcony. *No one's here.*

Connor retrieved the travel bag and checked the suitcase. The cardboard was intact.

He breathed a sigh of relief. The disc was still in its hiding place.

The silence shattered when the phone rang.

"Connor, how good to reach you," Paola Del Rubin's cheery voice was on the line. "I've asked my driver to stop at your hotel. There's no sense in your taking a taxi. You can ride to dinner with me. Come down to the lobby. I'll be there in a few minutes."

Something's happened. And it doesn't sound good. There was no planned dinner for that evening.

"Thank you, Paola. You're very kind. I'll be in the lobby in the next few minutes."

Connor checked his pockets to make sure he has his wallet and passport.

Connor took the disc out of its hiding space, slid it into his inside breast pocket, then tossed the bag on the floor.

He patted his pocket. *Wherever I go, it goes.*

Paola was waiting in the lobby. She smiled as he approached and reached to shake his hand. When he grasped her right hand, she reached up with her left and gently tugged his head toward her.

Her lips brushed his cheek. "You must leave as soon as possible," she whispered. "They have Manuel." She released his hand and gestured toward the door. "We shouldn't keep the others waiting."

Juan maneuvered the heavy evening traffic.

Paola closed the glass partition between the seats and turned the radio a little louder.

She put her hand over her upper lip. "Manuel didn't return to work after siesta yesterday," Paola whispered. "And, he never showed up at work today. There's word on the street he's been captured and is in the Modella Prison. He knows too much. And, he's made his opposition to Noriega known."

"I met him at La Plaza several nights ago. He passed some information to me."

"La Plaza? Why would he pick such a public place?"

Connor gave a little shrug. "He was sure no one would recognize him."

"If that's the reason they've arrested him, you're in danger. Now there's no question. You must leave Panama. They'll pick you up as soon as they figure out who you are. No matter how strong Manuel is, he'll break under their torture. Everyone eventually breaks."

"Someone went through my clothes and papers today."

"We have to assume they've broken Manuel." Tears filled her eyes. "They are incredibly cruel."

Connor nodded. "Where are we going?"

"To have dinner with friends."

After a long and circuitous route, Juan pulled through a back gate to Isobel and Roberto's house.

Stuart
The Town Dock

Stuart stood. "Let's get a table and order some dinner." William took Anne's arm.

Chance, their favorite waiter, seated them at a table overlooking the dock and took their dinner orders. Stuart and William asked for refills on their drinks. Anne requested a glass of merlot.

Anne reached across the table to grasp their hands. "My life is spinning out of control."

"Because of Herb?"

"No, he's only the annoying addition to the problems."

Stuart took a deep breath. His feelings of discomfort increased. "Was there a trigger point?"

Anne nodded, "Nothing's been the same since I had dinner with Connor on Thursday evening. Our dinner was great. We did a lot of reminiscing. Then the evening started to fall apart. Connor didn't come back to my place. Not even for a cup of tea. He always comes in for a cup of tea. Even when he's not able to stay. It's a tradition." She swiped at a tear threatening the corner of one eye. "Every date we've had since high school ended with a cup of tea. He'd take me home from a date, and we'd go to the kitchen and have a cup of tea before he went home."

Chance arrived at the table with their drinks. "Are you ready for dinner?"

William shook his head. "Keep the plates warm for another ten minutes, please, Chance." He waited until their server was out of ear shot. "Take another deep breath, Anne."

"That night, Connor hailed a taxi as soon as we reached the street. He kissed me goodnight and gave the driver a pile of bills and my address. When I opened the door to my house – I got chills. It felt like someone had been in my house." Anne crossed her arms and shivered.

Stuart stared at Anne's hands. *Even telling the story frightens her.* "Was anything missing?"

Anne shook her head. "No, but *someone* rummaged around my house. The pillows on the couch were at the wrong angle. One of the rugs had the corner flipped up, and the clothes in my closet were all squished together."

Anne shivered again.

"Did you call the police?"

"What could I say? My pillows are crooked? They'd think I was a nut job."

"How's everything else going?"

"My professional life is upside down. One patient's father is threatening me. Another patient has fantasies that are getting more and more violent. I'm afraid he's about to tip over the edge and…?"

"Wait," Stuart held his hands up, "You were threatened by the father of one of your patients?"

"Yes, he's from South American. He's very rich."

"You have a patient whose father is a wealthy man from South America?" All the gauges of Stuart's training, and his experience in South America, were in the red zone.

William whispered in Anne's ear, "How did he get his fortune?"

Anne whispered back. "Gossip says he grows and processes something illegal on his ranch."

"Let me guess. You haven't reported the threat to the police, either."

"I can't. I would have to give the police the man's name. It would be a breach of patient confidentiality."

Carcel Modella Prison

The room smelled of blood, sweat, urine, and fear.

"Señor D'Ormondo, who did you meet in La Plaza?" An ugly laugh and a snarl. "I knew you were not to be trusted. I told them you would sell out to the highest bidder. Who did you meet? Who did you give the information to?"

Manuel was naked and bound to a heavy three-legged chair with a high back. His arms pulled so tight they dislocated his shoulders.

The bones in his legs had multiple fractures. Both collar bones shattered. His left lung collapsed. His chest and abdomen purple.

Manuel was beyond answering. His face was destroyed. He had burns on his neck from a rope intermittently yanked backward. His larynx was crushed. Manuel couldn't talk even if he wanted to.

He was past pain and past feeling.

"Señor, you don't have much longer to live. When you meet your creator, you will have to tell him you couldn't complete your objective."

The man paced. Nervous. Angry. "We'll find your friend. His fate will be much like yours. And you can be sure our hospitality will extend far longer than two days." The voice was low. Cruel.

The executioner's eyes narrowed, he picked up a thick plank and gauged its weight. He slammed the plank into Manuel's neck and face. The torture continued. The man smashed the plank into Manuel's head and neck again and again until there was only pulp. A gurgle. There was a spurt of blood. Then all was silent.

The torturer's gut clamped. *How could this rich piece of shit not break?* He continued to smash the plank against Manuel's body until Manuel's ribs caved in. The crunch of bone-shattering and breaking reached a malignant core in the man that seemed to satisfy some inner loathing. He destroyed Manuel's abdomen and legs. Anger spent, he threw the plank against the wall and stormed out of the room.

"Dump what's left of that piece of shit in the street tonight. Throw him on top of his clothes. Make sure his identification papers are in one of the pockets."

Who did he meet in La Plaza?

Connor
Isobel and Roberto's House

Isobel and Roberto greeted Connor and Paola.

Isobel took Connor's arm. "Come, Connor, our guests are anxious to talk to you."

John Droges offered his hand. "Hello, Connor, good to see you."

From across the room, Eduardo Riesman smiled and nodded.

Guests told amusing stories about children and grandchildren. They shared the latest White Tail gossip—small complaints about the increasing inability to purchase luxuries.

There was no mention regarding Connor's situation, Manuel, or the unrest in Panama.

After dinner, the group gathered for cordials and coffee in the library. The massive doors closed. Music muted the conversations.

Isobel, her voice low and underlined with tension, addressed the gathering. "Manuel's been arrested and taken to Modella. Connor must return to the United States in the morning. He needs to know about the Panamanian drug trade, Noriega's weaknesses, and anything else that will convince the United States government to intervene. I hope he'll be able to deliver our information to people who can help."

John Droges was the first to speak up. "Ken Muse was caught. Someone successfully traced his pirate radio signal. He's in Modella Prison. My informants tell me Muse is still alive."

"They'll kill him eventually. If the stories we hear regarding the torture are close to the truth, death will come as a relief." Droges took a deep breath. "Manuel was taken to Modella."

Connor nodded to Droges. "What information do you have about Modella?"

"The Panamanian military took over operations of the prison after the failed coup in October. The stories of cruelty and torture grow more gruesome every day."

A gnawing concern gripped Connor's gut.

"Noriega considers himself quite a ladies' man." Isobel shivered. "He tried to seduce me. His behavior is worse than the crude behavior of an uneducated peasant."

"I'm told he uses cocaine when he has sex."

"His women must love money."

"Well, why else would they sleep with him?"

"One of his mistresses lives near the airport."

"She seems to be his favorite."

Paola interrupted, "Stop gossiping. We don't have much time. Give Connor our information."

"Several years ago, I saw the plans for the prison," Eduardo Riesman said in a whisper. He spoke in soft tones and described the prison in specific detail.

Each person had information for Connor.

"President Endara approved drug trafficking. He created the cover corporations."

"The drug cartels made him a wealthy man."

"Endara's weak," Paola noted.

"He is easily influenced."

"His daughter's driving him," Roberto added. "But we can't count him out completely. He has capable vice presidents who could be valuable assets."

"Endara's planning to get married. His daughter will be over-ruled by the headstrong young woman about to become Endara's wife."

"If they take out Noriega, Endara is next in line to become president."

"He'll agree to serve. He loves power."

The entire group nodded in agreement.

Riesman joined the conversation.

"The American government helped to finance Endara's campaign. I've never understood why the State Department supported Endara." He waved the concern away. "Manuel had been looking into connections to the Panamanian International Bank. He gathered proof of Noriega's involvement in moving drugs and money through Panama."

The mention of Manuel brought everyone back to the problem at hand.

"Connor, you must leave Panama immediately. You can't wait until morning. If you stay, you'll end up as another martyr to our struggle." Riesman's tone left no room for argument. "You'll be found dead outside a tavern or in an alley." He shrugged, "The newspapers will report another American businessman who had his throat slit by a disgruntled whore."

Riesman's remarks seemed to open flood gates of information. Connor listened carefully and prayed he could retain it all.

The guests left individually. Each wished Connor God-speed.

"Thank you again, Isobel, Roberto. Hope to see you soon."

"Sooner than you think. You'll be staying here. You can't return to your hotel."

Connor shook his head. "No – I'll…"

Isobel held up her hand. "No arguments. You'll be safe here."

Ora
The Town Dock
The Same Evening

Ora sat at the bar with his back to Anne, William, and Stuart. The two strangers sat at a table close to Anne and her friends. Ora looked out over the water and listened to the conversation.

"Dr. Anne," Rosie exclaimed, "it's so good to see you two nights in a row. What brings you out during the week? Taking a vacation?"

Anne nodded. "Work has been a real bear. I feel as if I've already put in a full week's work. I needed some time away from the office."

The two strangers nursed their drinks.

At about nine o'clock, Anne, William, and Stuart left the Town Dock.

One of the men following Anne threw several ten-dollar bills on the bar. He gestured to his partner. They walked out of the restaurant less than a minute later.

Ora paid his bill and strolled out to the parking lot. He moved into the shadow of the trees surrounding the Town Dock and waited. Anne and her friends chatted and laughed. They walked across the parking lot to Mulberry Street.

The two suspicious men remained in their car.

Ora leaned back against his tree and waited.

Forty-five minutes later, Stuart and William walked Anne across the parking lot to her car.

"Please stay with us tonight." William stood with his hand on Anne's car door, "We don't like the idea of you being alone at the cottage."

"I need the solitude."

William shook his head and started to object.

"I'll lock the door; I won't open it to anyone. I'll be fine," Anne assured them. "But thanks, I appreciate the offer."

Anne kissed each man on the cheek, opened the car door, then slid behind the steering wheel. William closed the door. She waved good night and started up Mulberry Street.

Seconds later, the sedan started. The driver pulled out of the parking lot and drove less than a car length behind Anne.

Ora's car was parked on Water Street, a block away. He casually walked to his car, drove along Water Street, and turned toward the highway when he got to East Chew Avenue.

The Captain's right. Doctor Anne is *in danger.*

Ora saw Anne turn left off the highway.

The sedan turned right and parked in front of the Post Office.

Ora continued down the highway, drove over the Oak Creek Bridge, and pulled into a dirt road about a half-mile down the road. He extinguished his car lights, waited a few minutes, then backed out onto the highway, and turned on his headlights. Ora retraced his route over the Oak Creek Bridge and passed Anne's driveway without slowing down.

About a half-mile down the road, there was a large empty lot.

The trees and shrubs lining the highway grew in profusion—a gravel driveway cut through the brush toward the water's edge.

Ora continued until he reached a curve in the highway, doused off his car lights, and turned into the gravel drive.

He stopped close to the cove's shoreline. An old boathouse was on his right.

He parked and locked his car.

Once he was in the shadow of the boathouse overhang, he walked along the waterfront toward Anne's cottage.

Anne
The Next Morning
April 22, 1989

Anne woke early. A rim of bright red dawn lined the trees on the eastern edge of the cove.

She fixed a tray with cereal and coffee, then put on a heavy robe, and carried the tray out to the screened porch. The sun rose higher in the sky and turned the lake and the sky beautiful shades of pink and blue. Swans glided by Anne's dock on their way to the edge of the cove.

Anne sipped her coffee. She loved watching the sunrise and wondered if she should move to Newcomb and commute to work. It was tempting.

The phone rang.

Anne walked back into the cottage and picked up the receiver.

"Good Morning, Dr. Anne."

"Cindy? What's the matter?"

"Señor Empañada insists you keep your appointment with Helena."

Anne rubbed her forehead. "Tell him I'm out of town for a family emergency."

"I tried. Señor Empañada laughed and said he knew better."

Anne caught her breath and pulled the curtain to the side. *Does he have someone watching me?*

"Dr. Anne?"

"I'm here. No point in trying to dissuade Señor Empañada. Call Helena and tell her to come in at her regular time. I'll be there as soon as I can."

"Dr. Anne, Dr. Smithfield's looking for you, as well."

Ora
The Same Morning

The night had been long and cold. Ora learned years earlier to block out the discomfort of foul weather. He could remain quiet and unmoving for hours. He knelt behind a bush and watched the sunrise.

When he noticed activity in the house, Ora stretched the stiffness from his legs and walked through the brush. He found a vantage point where he could keep the cottage and the sedan in his vision.

The vehicle had not moved. Both men still sat in the front seat, smoking, their eyes on the entrance to Anne's driveway.

Anne, dressed in a business suit, carried her trench coat and briefcase to the car. She drove down the lane and turned toward Easton.

The driver of the sedan started the car and followed her.

Ora ran back to his vehicle. He had both cars in his sight by the time they got to Wye Mills.

Anne stayed on Highway 50 and crossed the Annapolis Bay Bridge. "She must be on her way to the office."

Ora pulled into the Outlet Center parking lot in Queenstown, then turned and went to Newcomb.

No one can see the cottage from the road. And, there's no direct view of the walkway or front door from any of the neighbor's houses.

Ora noted the damage to the screen and was pleased that there was no evidence of damage to the door or windows.

His first concern was how easy it was to break into Anne's house.

A photograph of Connor standing on the deck outside caught his attention. *The Captain looks happy and relaxed.*

He noticed another picture of Connor on the dresser in Anne's bedroom. *I didn't know the Captain could ski.*

When Ora walked around the outside of the cottage, he noted globs of sand on the porch and at least three different sets of shoe prints.

Paola
Isobel and Roberto's House
The Next Morning
April 23, 1989

Paola called Juan and asked him to bring the small van to the door. The vehicle would not attract attention.

"Please take a circuitous route to the airport," she said as she slid into the vehicle.

Paola had arranged a seat for a 'Joseph Snavely' on an early morning flight to Miami.

Connor and Paola got out of the van at the curb and walked to the check-in counter.

Connor pushed a passport across the counter toward the clerk. "Good morning. You should have a ticket waiting for me."

The clerk looked at the picture ID, smiled, and handed Mr. Joseph Snavely's ticket to Connor. "Have a good trip, sir."

"Thank you."

The clerk immediately turned to the baggage handler. "El Hombre's battalion is at the screening point," the clerk announced in a stage whisper. "They're looking for someone."

"Si, I was told they are looking for some Cuban."

The men, intent on their conversation, barely glanced at Connor.

Paola walked Connor to the screening area. He paid his exit tax, had his passport checked, and sent his carry-on through the magnetometer.

Paola undid the top two buttons of her blouse as they neared the screening point.

Three serious-looking men worked the entrance to the departure lounge. A customs man, a man who focused his attention on the x-ray machine, and a third man, eyes narrowed, who watched everyone moving through the door.

The woman in front of Connor and Paola turned to her companion. "The clerk said they're looking for a killer," she murmured. "They're sure he's alone."

Paola undid another button.

Connor handed his passport to the agent.

Paola adjusted her blouse to expose her cleavage. Her movements distracted the man who was supposed to be watching the x-ray machine.

He stared at Paola and licked his lips.

She raised her eyebrows and moved seductively.

The screener ignored the x-ray machine.

Paola leaned even further over the agent's desk. She gave him another inviting smile, then turned toward Connor.

"My darling," her voice was husky. "You were *so* good last night," she purred, "I'm still on fire."

Paola pulled Connor toward her and pressed her pelvis to his. "I burn for you." Her hand moved down his leg. She ground against Connor. "How can you leave me now?"

Connor moved his hand down her tight skirt, grabbed her buttocks, and pulled her even tighter against his groin.

The screeners watched.

She gave Connor a seductive smile. "Es usted duro?"

The men's eyes went wide. Their lips parted in surprise. "She's too hot for a gringo."

Connor mumbled, "I'm not sure I want to leave."

"If you don't, we're both in trouble." Her tongue grazed his neck.

Connor responded to one more passionate kiss, picked up his carry-on bag, and walked toward the boarding area.

Paola smoothed her skirt, fiddled with one of the buttons on her blouse then turned and smiled at the three men, "I long for him every minute he's away. I've never had such a talented lover."

Anne

Anne glanced in her rearview mirror. *There's a black car behind me again.*

Despite the increased traffic, the sedan was only two car lengths behind her at the Bay Bridge toll booth.

At M Street, the car was still there. She turned left on Thirtieth Street. So did the sedan. When Anne pulled into the Institute's parking garage, the vehicle continued toward the Whitehurst Freeway.

She parked her car and walked to the stairway oblivious to her surroundings.

Herb stepped in front of her and blocked the doorway. "I thought I told you to call off your goon."

Anne's head snapped up. "What?" Her heart seemed to stop, then beat double time. Her anger immediately flared. "Get out of my way. I distinctly remember telling you to leave me alone."

"Don't act so innocent. You know who I'm talking about. You hired a thug to work me over on Monday night."

She took a deep breath and sighed. "I have nothing to do with anyone following you. And, I didn't hire anyone to work you over."

"Your **friend** attacked me outside the church."

"What friend?" She shook her head. "What church?"

"Don't be naïve." Herb narrowed his eyes and took a step closer.

Anne stepped to the side and started to walk around him. "You're not making any sense. My patient will be here any moment."

Herb grabbed her arm. "He attacked me at Christ Church on Monday."

She pulled her arm free. "I went into Christ Church to pray. I was the only person in the church. You weren't there."

"I didn't go inside. I didn't have a chance. Your goon attacked me before I got to the door."

Anne moved toward the stairs.

Herb blocked her way. "I was in the churchyard, Miss Smarty-pants."

"What did you call me?"

Herb brushed off her comment. "Tell your friend he won't be so lucky if he tries one of his tricks again. Next time he'll get a bullet for his trouble."

"A bullet? Where did you get a gun?"

"Mumsie's attic." Herb rolled his eyes and huffed. "Father brought a Lugar back from Germany. The bullets were there, too."

"Does your father know you have his gun?"

"Of course not. I was told **never** to touch Daddy's precious gun. He fancies himself a great hero of the war."

"You don't know the first thing about guns."

"What's there to know? You pull the trigger and a bullet comes out. I won't even have to aim. I'll shoot him at short range."

"The gun's been in the attic since the end of World War Two? Has the gun been fired in all these years? Has it ever been cleaned?"

Herb put his hands on his hips. "Dr. Anne, the big gun expert. Your friend's a big dumb jerk. He isn't even an American."

"Herb, get away from the door. I'm tired of listening to your ridiculous ranting."

"Give your friend a message from me." Herb reached into his pocket and brought out the weapon.

"He'll have *this* to contend with if he tries anything again."

"I have a better idea. I've got an appointment in a few minutes. But I have some time this afternoon. You're right. I think you and I should have a little talk with Mumsie."

"What?"

"I'll call her as soon as I get to my office. Where do you think your parents would like to meet us for dinner?"

Herb pocketed the gun. He shook his head. "No, no. You don't want to do that."

"Oh, yes I do, I've had more than enough of your threats. If you hear from Mumsie in the meantime tell her, she can pick the place." Anne walked around him, opened the door, and ran up the stairs.

Connor
April 23, 1989

Connor slumped into a window seat and fastened the seat belt. He couldn't relax. The events of the past few days cycled in his mind.

He wondered if he would have been better off by going to the American Zone for refuge.

After considering all the pros and cons, he decided he made the right choice.

Connor willed his muscles to relax and checked off the lessons learned.

The Panamanian military will fight.

The businessmen will support a new Panamanian president.

Connor felt his tension gradually melting away.

He jolted awake when the pilot's crackly intercom voice announced their initial descent into Miami.

Connor looked at his watch and breathed a sigh of relief as he exited the jetway. He was always relieved to be back in the United States. Especially tonight.

Bags from his flight had already been removed from the baggage carousel and stacked against the wall. Two dogs were climbing over the stacked suitcases, undoubtedly looking for drugs. Customs agents watched as people claimed their bags and head for the long lines to clear customs.

Even though it was mid-March, the air-conditioned terminal didn't dissipate the Miami heat and humidity. The sun paid no heed to the calendar in this part of Florida.

Anne
The Institute

Anne opened Helena's chart. It was in total disarray.

The young woman was due to arrive in a few minutes.

She pressed the intercom button for Cindy's desk. "If you have a few minutes, please come to my office."

Cindy knocked on the door seconds later. "Yes, Dr. Anne?"

"Helena's file is a mess. It looks as if someone dropped the folder on the floor and just threw the pages back in."

Cindy's eyes flitted between the file and Anne's face. "I pulled the chart this morning after Señor Empañada's call. I never looked inside."

"Were the cleaning people here last night?"

Cindy shook her head. "Their usual cleaning days for our wing are Wednesday and Saturday."

Anne shook her head. "Please ask the record room if someone accidentally dropped the chart, or if anyone requested Helena's chart in the past few days."

Cindy nodded, "I'll let you know what they say."

Anne spread the papers on her desk and rearranged the chart.

Helena's poem is missing.

Cindy returned a few minutes later. "Dr. Anne, the file room people said they didn't disturb the chart. But the head librarian found this near the door when she came in this morning."

Cindy handed Anne a single piece of paper.

Helena's poem.

Anne stared at the paper. Her mind whirled with possibilities.

"Was the outer door locked when you came in this morning?"

"Yes."

"Any evidence that someone was in the suite last night?"

"No, Dr. Anne, everything looked normal when I came in this morning."

"This is all very strange. If anyone else notices irregularities, please let me know."

"You can count on it. I'm as mystified as you are." Cindy left Anne's office and closed the door behind her.

Anne sank into her chair and pulled out her keys to unlock her desk.

My desk is unlocked. I'm sure I locked it before I left yesterday.

Anne methodically checked all the drawers.

She breathed a sigh of relief. Her prescription pad was in the drawer. Even the spare change she used for the soda machine was there.

Cindy knocked and opened the office door. "Dr. Anne?"

Anne looked up. "Yes?"

She extended a leather-bound notebook to Anne. "Your address book was in the copy machine. It was face down on the **Q** page."

Connor

Connor glanced at the departure board. *Newark.* A flight was leaving in twenty minutes. He changed his ticket and carried his bag to the Newark departure gate.

He made the flight with seconds to spare and hoped the last-minute ticket change would confuse anyone who followed him.

Connor smiled at the agent checking tickets at the entrance to the gangway.

Killeen expects me in Washington for a debriefing today. Connor shrugged and shook his head. He formed an entirely different plan.

The plane banked to the left as it made its final descent into Newark.

The information Manuel gave him added a new wrinkle. It traced the flow of drug money and involved high-level American officials.

I'm carrying a bomb. Connor's skin prickled.

He took a few deep breaths. The feeling of danger persisted. Instead of heading for his office in New York, he asked the cab driver to take him to Penn Station in Newark.

"Humph! An hour wait for a five-dollar fare," the cab driver grumbled.

Lack of sleep and the tension of the past few days was taking its toll on Connor. He shook his head and blinked himself awake.

I can't afford to let down my guard.

Connor checked the Penn Station board. There were three options. The A train to Thirty-fourth Street in Manhattan, a train to the World Trade Center, or with a quick change in Jersey City, he could get to Thirty-third Street.

He chose the train to the World Trade Center.

Angela
One World Trade Center

Angela pushed back from her computer when Connor walked into the suite. Accustomed to Connor's erratic schedule, she'd learned long ago not to ask questions.

Connor rapped his knuckles on the edge of her desk in greeting and walked directly into his office.

She followed him.

He glanced up, "Any messages?"

"Several calls from representatives of Maersk. New Orleans wants you to help them with some kind of project. And someone named Mr. Oratchewski called. He wants you to call him immediately. He said it was important. I hope you know where to reach him. He didn't leave a number."

Angela pointed to a long line of stickies on his blotter. "And, there were more than a few other calls."

She crossed her arms. "Have you gotten any rest? You look like hell."

"A short nap on the plane, no real rest." He waved away her concern. "Did Killeen call? Any other government types?"

"Yeah, Mr. Donovan called."

Connor

Connor smiled. *Donovan called. It's gone up to the next level already.* Satisfaction settled in his gut. Donovan was one of the movers and shakers in the CIA, and he was rapidly moving up the chain.

He was concerned about the call from Ora. *I hope Anne's alright. He never calls me.*

Connor dialed Ora's private number, waited a few seconds, then included a few identifying numbers signaling 'urgent.'

Connor waited.

When his private phone rang, he grabbed the receiver and was relieved to hear Ora's deep voice.

"Welcome back, Captain. I've checked on Anne. She's okay now."

"Okay, now?" What the hell does that mean?"

"Several people are following Anne. It's beginning to look like a parade. One's a rich jerk. He's obsessed with her. Some guy she works with. My guess is he's an old boyfriend who can't accept the fact that she doesn't want to have anything to do with him. Yesterday it looked like he was going to hurt her. I sent him a message."

"What did you do?"

"Just scared him a little."

"Did that take care of the problem?"

"I think so – but there's more."

"Isn't that enough?

"She's one complicated lady. Professionals are following her. I had to use some techniques so they wouldn't notice me. The stupidity of the rich guy helps. He's gotten in their way a few times. For a while there, it was beginning to look like a traffic jam."

"Professionals?"

"Yeah. Anne's house has been searched a couple of times, and they're following her everywhere she goes. It looks like they're keeping track of her. I can't see any reason why."

Connor thought of the men who followed him in the Metro. "Describe them."

Gloria Casale

"They have pretty good builds—medium height. Look Hispanic. I was never close enough to hear them speak."

"I'll be in Washington tomorrow morning. I'll call you from the train on my way into town."

Angela plunked a steaming cup of coffee on his desk. "You need rest," she said and turned on her heel. "In case you didn't hear me before. You look like hell."

"Thanks for the cheering words of welcome." Connor laughed and waited for Angela to close the door. He dialed a second number.

A woman answered.

"Can you put me up for the night? I can't go back to my place, and I need some rest. I can't explain."

"So, what else's new? You can never explain. Do you still have a key?"

"Yes."

"You know where the spare bedroom is. Make yourself comfortable. I'm going to a cocktail party after work. Where'd you almost get yourself killed this time?"

"Maybe I'll be able to tell you – someday."

"I work with you on one mission and wind up patching you up forever. Your extra clothes are in the closet. There's food in the fridge."

Connor opened the desk drawer, located her key, and stared at his blank computer screen. He considered reviewing the disc. It felt like a lead weight.

He finally decided exhaustion was winning the game. He drained the last of the coffee, picked up his bag, and walked past Angela toward the door.

He knuckle rapped her desk.

"Good to see you too, Boss. Hope to hear from you soon. By the way, did I tell you, you look like hell?"

Herb

Herb paced outside Anne's office, waiting for Helena to leave. He was sweating profusely and muttering to himself.

The door cracked open. "Thank you, Dr. Damiano. I'll see you next week." Helena skirted around Herb and waved at Cindy on her way out of the office.

Herb waited. His stomach churned. He tapped on Anne's door.

"Come in." Anne was sitting at her desk; her hand was on the phone receiver. "Herb, I'm glad you're here. I was just about to call Mumsie. I'm sure you need to hear this as well."

"You probably won't reach Mumsie. She said she had a bridge date today."

"I'll call and leave her a message to call me back. This is far too important."

"What are you going to say to her?"

"I will let her know how intrusive you and she are in my life. I will tell her I have no intention of being a part of the Smithfield family. I will also inform her that I would rather lose my job than put up with you and your threats ever again."

"N-no. You don't have to do that. I'll tell her we're no longer dating."

"I don't think you can be trusted to give Mumsie that information. You have been lying to her for over a year."

"But-but ..." Tears streamed down Herb's face.

"I've had enough of you, enough of your lies, and enough of your threats."

"Anne ..."

"I don't want to hear another word. You can tell Mumsie she can call Director Frye. If he fires me, I'm sure I'll find work elsewhere."

Herb opened his mouth. No sound came out.

"Get out of my office."

Connor

Connor left One World Trade Center and walked to the Marriott Hotel. The doorman summoned a cab.

Elke's place can be a haven – for tonight.

He had the cab driver drop him off at the Lincoln Center for the Performing Arts. It was several blocks from Elke's apartment building. He walked a circuitous route to her apartment.

Connor rode to the penthouse level of a building that had a great view of Central Park. Her marble foyer opened into a large, well-appointed living room. Elke paid big bucks to have the place decorated.

As promised, there was plenty of food in the refrigerator. Connor hadn't had anything to eat since the dinner at Isobel's house. He made himself a ham and cheese sandwich.

He pulled the disk out of its hiding place. *What did Manuel know that cost him his life?"*

Elke's computer was in the study.

The room looked like a movie set. A large wooden desk dominated the room. A leather couch occupied the length of one wall. An oak bookcase stretched across another. Medical journals and fashion magazines lay on a table next to the sofa

He slid the disc into the computer. There were lists of bank accounts and transactions.

Connor scrutinized the information. It covered several years of transactions.

Connor had a flash of understanding. It was the history of money passing through accounts in several nations. Along with lists of the people associated with the accounts. He recognized some of the Columbian and Panamanian names.

There were American names too. It was a goldmine. As he scrolled down the list, he was surprised to see prominent names from Washington. Then he saw a name that caused him to stop scrolling.

Oh shit! If this guy's involved, I'm in real danger. Exhaustion was rapidly taking its toll.

Connor rummaged through the drawers of the desk. When he found what he wanted, he returned to the computer, copied the disc, and left the copy in the top right drawer of Elke's desk.

Connor put the original back in his jacket pocket.

His shoulder ached. And, he knew he needed sleep.

His clothes, left in the apartment months before, hung on a rack in the back of the closet. They'd been laundered and pressed. "Bless you, Elke."

A long hot shower relaxed his muscles. After he dried himself and put on the clean boxer shorts, he collapsed across the bed and fell into a deep sleep as the sun began to dip below Central Park.

Connor
The Next Morning
April 24, 1989

Connor woke to the smell of freshly brewed coffee. He pulled on a T-shirt and a pair of slacks and walked to the kitchen. There was a note on the counter next to the coffee maker.

'I'm off to early morning appointments. Keep me posted.'
Elke'd left a plate of cinnamon rolls and another note. *'Enjoy.'*

He polished off half the pot of coffee and two of the cinnamon rolls.

Connor boarded a Metro liner with just a few seconds to spare. He called Ora and asked him to be at the Union Station coffee shop.

When Connor left the train, he joined the crowd of impatient passengers flooding the station's escalators and stairs.

Most of the commuters disbursed rapidly through the large marble lobby. Connor strolled to the coffee shop and ordered a cup of coffee. He chose a table against the wall away from the flow of traffic. As soon as he sat down, Ora slid into a chair across the table from him.

"It didn't look like anyone was following you, Sir."

"Thanks for watching out for me."

Ora smiled, "I have good news. Your Anne has pictures of you in both her houses. And, it looks like she lives alone."

"I could have told you that."

"You asked me to check on her."

"I'm worried about the men who are following her."

"The guy who works in her building won't be bothering her again." Ora paused. "But the professionals look like bad news. They haven't tried to hurt her. They park out in front of the townhouse. They follow her to work and wait for her to leave in the evening. When she's at her cottage in Newcomb, they watch her movements from the post office parking lot across the street. They look Hispanic."

"Do you think they're waiting for someone to give the word to kill or capture her?"

Ora shook his head and shrugged his shoulders. "I don't know. There's no way to tell. It's a possibility, I guess."

"From your description, they sound like the guys who followed me the last time I was in DC. The guy that came inside and got on the escalator seemed dumber than a box of rocks."

"Do you think there's a connection?"

"I'm not sure. While I was in Panama, I picked up information about people high up in our government. Lots of dirty money coming from Panama. Lots of well-placed people in our government are shoveling the money into their bank accounts."

"If you have that kind of information, it will put you on the top of several shit lists. I thought you were down there to help the Panamanian businessmen. And, in your spare time, collecting information about their stance on the Noriega regime."

Connor nodded. "I was. Everything fell apart the last day I was there. My main contact was taken to Modella Prison. He was tortured and killed. They threw his physically unidentifiable body out in the street with his ID's attached. I was lucky to get out of Panama alive." Connor took a deep breath and slowly exhaled. "Thanks for the information and watching out for Anne."

"I'll be leaving the States in less than a week. They have my report on the Panamanian military. I've been debriefed. They're talking about sending me back to Germany. Some kind of problem is growing there."

"I hoped you could spend at least a few more days around here."

"I'll stretch it out as long as I can, Captain." A look of consternation flashed across Ora's face. "Guess who I saw in St. Michaels."

Connor laughed. "William and Stuart?"

Ora looked even more puzzled. "You've seen our old friends from Bogotá?"

"That's them. William and Stuart. Those are their new names."

Ora nodded. "They walked into the restaurant and asked for Anne. I almost fell off the barstool."

"I had a similar reaction. When Anne introduced me to them, we all had a hard time making believe we'd never met before."

Ora left the coffee shop. Connor refilled his coffee and watched the flow of human traffic through Union Station. He reviewed his options.

I need to call Donovan. Connor shifted in his chair and took another bite of the sweet roll. *And I better call Elke.*

Connor made his first call. "Donovan, meet me at the J. W. Marriott. Be there as quick as you can."

"You need to come in. It's not safe for you out there. Lots of talk on the street about you."

"Can't. I have at least one pressing problem. But there's something I must hand over to you. Be there as soon as possible."

Fred Worthington
State Department

Fred leaned back and smiled. Tonight was going to be another rung up on the social ladder. He and his wife were going to a posh dinner party. He would be rubbing shoulders with the rich and famous.

Fred basked in the thrill of anticipation.

He scanned his hands. *I should get a manicure.*

The light on his private line flashed.

"Worthington here."

"Buenos tardes, Fredrico."

The voice belonged to a man who could destroy him.

Fred's feelings of accomplishment evaporated. He shivered and forced a light tone.

"Buenos tardes. Are you in Washington?" Fred hoped he kept the fear from his voice.

"No, I'm calling from my home."

Palpable relief eased Fred's muscles.

"Manuel D'Ormondo is dead." The caller's voice was a low growl.

Fred's gut clenched.

"They threw his almost unidentifiable body on the street outside of a whorehouse."

Fred cleared his throat but was unable to utter a sound.

The gruff voice continued, "D'Ormando turned his information over to someone. An American man who visited Panama this week."

Quinlan. Fred could feel the liquid in his gut roil.

"Unfortunately, D'Ormando's contact was able to get out of Panama before we could discuss the situation with him. We fear he has enough information to take us all down."

"And what would you have me do?" Fred voiced sarcasm. "I'm not one of your strong-arm henchmen." Fred closed his eyes and bowed his head. *Smart mouth replies will get me killed.*

The caller laughed. "We wouldn't trust *you* with any job that important. Get off your pampered ass. Find out where Quinlan is, or your future will not be promising."

Fred knew the man would keep his promise. The man's associates knew where Fred lived, where he banked, where he played golf. The cartel owned Fred.

"What do you want me to do?"

"Find out why Quinlan was in Panama. And, more importantly, tell us where he is now."

Fred trembled. His caller was powerful and ruthless. No negotiations. No compromise.

The cartel boss continued. "We're keeping an eye on one of his friends. If all else fails, we can use her as bait to reel him in."

Anne
The Institute

Anne was ready to see her first patient of the day. Her phone rang.

"Dr. Damiano, this is Mateo Empañada. I'm pleased with my daughter's progress. She seems well enough to return home."

"Señor Empañada, Helena *is* doing much better. But much of her improvement is the result of the medication she's taking."

"We will leave for Columbia at the end of the school term."

"I'd be hesitant to send her back this soon. Her progress has been good. But, she's *far* from recovered. She could have a significant relapse."

"We will leave for Columbia on June fourth."

"Please, Señor, it would be better to wait another semester. She's still afraid."

There was a pause.

"I am a reasonable man. I will compromise. You may have one additional month. She will leave with me on July fourth."

Connor
Washington, DC

Connor exited the red line at Metro Center and walked to Gallery Place. He strolled through the mall and used the store windows to watch for anyone who could be following him. Connor wandered through a few of the shops before heading toward the J.W. Marriot Hotel.

Donovan lounged against the mezzanine railing. He seemed focused on the lobby

Connor sidled up from the hallway behind Donovan. *Has he been out of the field so long he's lost his edge?*

A millisecond later, Donovan spun around and grabbed Connor's arm.

Connor caught his breath, then chuckled, "I didn't think you saw me coming."

"You should know better." Donovan shook his head. "Good to see you, lad. What's with the price on your head? You seem to be getting more valuable by the minute."

Connor told Donovan about the disc and his narrow escape from Panama.

"So, the cartel is after the information D'Ormondo passed to you." It wasn't a question.

"Looks that way. I had a chance to scan the disc this morning. It traces drug money from South America to Panama and Washington. People in our government are involved big time. Worthington's one of them. The Panama operation is compromised."

Donovan moved away from the railing, walked to a small seating area, and gestured for Connor to sit. "No doubt about it. Worthington's been at every briefing and debriefing." Donovan chose a chair with a full view of the mezzanine. "You need to come in."

"I've got a few things to check on first. I'm hoping I can get everything taken care of in twenty-four hours."

Donovan shook his head. "You know the drill. You get debriefed first. We need specific information on the Panamanian shipping industry."

"What about the drug dealing and the transfer of money?"

"Not my problem. Another group will handle those problems. Our mission is to take out Pineapple Face. You have one day. Be in my office tomorrow morning."

Connor handed Donovan a roll of film.

"What's this?"

"Pictures. Couldn't pass up the opportunity. The Panama City Marriott has an excellent landing zone directly across the street. A straight run in from the sea."

"See you at nine A.M. sharp."

"Do you want the disc?"

"No. Bring it with you. Whoever's assigned to follow up on the information will probably get in touch with you in a day or two."

Donovan picked up a newspaper from the table next to him and snapped it open.

Connor exited the shopping mall, circled back to the J.W. Marriott, slipped into a phone booth, and dialed a New York number.

"Let me guess," Elke said. "Thanks for the food and bed. You're gone again. Now, what do you want?"

"Check the right top drawer of your desk. There's a computer disc labeled 'Floor plan.' Get it to Paul Garcia ASAP. His office is in Foley Square. Tell him the CD is from me. Don't read it no matter how tempted you might be."

Anne
The Same Day

Anne smiled and lowered the phone receiver. *Trish and Lenny have just landed at BWI. It'll be good to see them again.*

She walked to the kitchen and scanned the food in the refrigerator. *Eggs, milk, coffee, OJ.* She opened a cabinet. *Enough snacks. Booze?* A quick check of the cupboard over the stove. *Bourbon for Lenny. Vodka for Trish. Sour mix, vermouth.* The wine rack was well stocked with reds and whites. *Can't think of anything else.*

Anne straightened and stretched. *That should be more than enough to get us through the weekend. What else?* She glanced at the clock. *By the time their luggage comes in, and they pick up the rental car, it'll be six-thirty.*

She ran up the stairs, opened the linen closet, then changed her mind. *They'll be more comfortable in my bedroom. I'll move my stuff to the guest room for the weekend.*

Anne changed the sheets and put out clean towels. A last look around was all she had time for before the doorbell rang.

Anne greeted her guests with a huge smile. "I'm so glad you're here." She hugged Trish. "It's been way too long."

Trish and Anne had been best friends in medical school.

Lenny was the Chief of Urology at Northwestern. He was meeting with colleagues at George Washington School of Medicine.

The three friends sat by the fireplace in Anne's living room. The cheery blaze took off the chill of the spring air.

"Anne, why haven't you found someone to marry?" Lenny grabbed a chunk of Jarlsberg cheese.

Anne, a bit shaken by the bluntness of the question, gave a quick shrug of her shoulders. "I guess it's because I haven't gotten a proposal from anyone I'd want to spend the rest of my life with."

The confusion on Lenny's face prompted Trish to jump in. She elbowed him. "Anne means there's someone she wants to marry. But he hasn't asked her - yet."

"He hasn't, and he won't." Sadness tinged Anne's answer.

Still confused, Lenny asked, "Who *is* this shadowy figure? Why haven't any of us met him?"

"You both met him. A long time ago." Anne shook her head. "You just didn't know it was him. He loves me. But he'll never marry me."

"Maybe it's time for you to find someone else. How wonderful can this guy be if he doesn't realize what a prize you are? You have a life to live. What are you waiting for?"

"I don't know. I just wait. Twenty years of habit is hard to break." Anne passed the tray of French bread and triple cream brie to Lenny.

"Twenty years?"

Anne sighed. "Yes, twenty years. We were childhood friends. We went steady in high school. Then we grew apart. During college, we dated off and on. He didn't seem to have much time for me."

"Another woman?"

Anne clamped her lips together. "I don't think so – I – don't know – Maybe – but there are a few other factors as well. I went to Rutgers University in Newark, and he went to St. Peter's in Jersey City."

"Newark and Jersey City are not all **that** far apart."

Anne chose not to respond directly to Lenny's statement. "There were more than a few complications. Our last date, he took me to a coffee shop in Newark to meet some of his friends. They were horrible. As soon as Connor left the table, they started in on me." Anne dropped her chin to her chest. The pain of that night never faded. "Their comments were ugly. "Common people go to Rutgers Newark. Rutgers standards were far below those of St. Peter's." She got a faraway look in her eyes. "They said no girl from Garwood could hold a candle to the girls Connor had the opportunity to meet at St. Peter's. One of them made a seemingly off-handed remark about Connor dating a debutant from New York."

Tears welled in Anne's eyes. "When I finally had enough, I said a guy from Cornell invited me to come to Ithaca for Spring Weekend. He was someone I knew from high school. I'd started to date him during the Christmas break. He'd asked me to wear his pin."

"You were pinned?"

"Briefly. I pulled the Lambda Chi Alpha fraternity pin from my purse and said something about my being good enough for someone at Cornell." A deep breath, "Just then, Connor returned to the table and saw the pin. I grabbed the pin, stood, and asked him to take me home."

Anne blinked and rubbed her forehead.

Trish and Lenny sat, wide-eyed and silent.

"I didn't hear from Connor for a long time after that night. Every once in a while, I'd call his house. He'd sound friendly, like his old self. But he never picked up on the hints about going out."

"The guy from Cornell was a total jerk. He couldn't hold a candle to Connor. I gave him back his pin and never saw him again after Spring Weekend."

Lenny refilled the wine glasses. "When was the next time you saw Connor?"

"Every once in a while, I'd bump into him in Newark. He'd tell me about the debutante he was dating and how his future was going to be perfect because of her wealthy daddy. I'd tell him about whatever guy I was dating at the time. We spent a lot of time hurting each other."

"Sounds like an excess of pride – on both sides," Lenny grumbled.

"I got accepted to medical school. You guys know the story from there. Medical school, residencies in Peds and Psych."

Trish closed her eyes and shook her head. "Then she got a Master of Science in Public Health – just for the fun of it."

Lenny's brow wrinkled. He glanced at Anne, "So, my overachieving friend, where was 'Mister Wonderful' all this time?"

"Law school, then in the military. Intelligence." She sighed. "The army changed him. He came home from his training at Ft. Benning and told me not to wait for him. He was on his way to Nam. He said he probably wouldn't make it back from his assignment."

Trish
The Next Morning
April 25, 1989

Trish walked Lenny to the front door. "Bye, Honey," Trish yawned. "How come doctors go on vacation and still start their day at six-thirty in the morning?"

He gave her a hug and a quick kiss on the cheek. "I'm off to learn the latest in Urology. Can you imagine a more exciting day?" He opened the door.

Anne fished in her pocket, "Here's a key, Len, if you're partying with your buddies, we'll probably beat you home. But just in case, you'll be able to get in. Trish and I are going to stop at the cottage in Newcomb. Then I'll take her shopping in St. Michaels. And we'll have dinner with some friends at the Town Dock."

"Thanks, Anne. I was hoping to come back to make a few phone calls when today's meetings are over. I need to check up on a few patients." He held up the key. "This will help. I don't know where my group wants to go for dinner."

A few hours later, Anne and Trish were on their way to Newcomb. The commuter traffic to through Annapolis was unusually heavy.

Anne flashed her friend a glance. "How'd you guys sleep last night?"

"Like logs. Your bed is *so* comfortable. Thank you so much."

"I thought you would like the privacy of the attached bathroom." Anne glanced in the rear-view mirror. A black sedan was behind her. "Damn."

Trish's head jerked up. She glanced at the road ahead. "What's the matter? What did we forget?"

"We haven't forgotten anything. Don't turn around." Anne shook her head. "A car has been following me for days. I think it's behind me again."

Trish looked into the side mirror. There were several cars in their lane. "Which one?"

"The black sedan."

Trish flipped down the visor to see if the mirror would give her a better look at the traffic behind them.

"There are lots of black sedans out there." She turned to look at Anne. "Why would someone be following you?"

"I don't know. Funny things have been happening."

"Funny things?"

"For about a month I was getting threatening phone calls. So, I got an unlisted number. Then one of the men I work with and dated briefly over a year ago started stalking me. I'm fairly sure I've taken care of that problem."

"Fairly sure?" Anne nodded, "I can't be absolutely sure. Yesterday he accused me of having someone beat him up. It looks like someone else is out there following him following me. And, that damn black sedan is always one or two car lengths behind me."

"Does the creep from work drive a black sedan?"

"Herb wouldn't be caught dead driving a nondescript, black sedan. He wouldn't even use a black sedan to go to the Mc Donald's to order a Big Mac. Second thought – he wouldn't be caught dead at Mc Donald's. Herb drives an expensive sports car."

"This Herb-guy told you somebody beat him up?"

"He said a 'big goon' beat him up and told him to stay away from me. Herb did have some scratches and bruises on his face. I have no idea how credible his story is."

Trish's eyebrows knit together. "Do you think the 'big goon' drives the black sedan?"

"I guess that's possible."

"Is Mister Wonderful a big guy?"

"No, he's average height and average build, and no one would ever describe him as a big goon. And his name is Connor. I'll show you his picture when we get to the cottage. You might remember him."

"Okay, so you've eliminated Connor from the list of goons." Trish flipped up the visor and watched the side mirror. "Do you think you're in danger?"

"I don't think so. I know someone searched my house several days ago. Nothing's missing. A few things were out of place."

"Are you sure?" Trish murmured.

"Pretty sure. It doesn't happen every day, but a couple of times this week, I've gotten a creepy feeling when I walk into my house after work. It's like spiders crawling across my neck." Anne maneuvered through the traffic on New York Avenue. "And, somehow, someone broke into the Institute, rifled through one of my patient charts, and copied pages from my address book."

"People are following you? Breaking and entering? Obscene telephone calls? Have you called the police? You have to assume you're in danger."

"What am I going to tell the police? There's a guy from work stalking me who says he *thinks* I hired someone to beat him up? I *think* my house was broken into and searched?"

"You're a respected physician. Surely, they'll listen to what you say. It's not like it was just one incident."

Anne stared straight ahead. "No broken windows. I didn't see any evidence that someone jimmied the doors."

Both women were silent for a few minutes

Tears glistened in Anne's eyes. She pulled a tissue from her purse. "The press would have a field day. I can just see the headlines in the Washington Post. Famous Shrink Stalked. Confidential Files not so confidential."

Trish
Tidewater Inn
Easton, Maryland
April 25, 1989

"What a quaint place!" Trish glanced around the dining room of the Tidewater Inn. Only a few tables had diners.

A few minutes later, two men entered the restaurant and requested a table across the room from the women.

"Easton never moved into the twentieth century. The town still hasn't moved too far out of the nineteenth century. I'm not sure how long it will last. Fast food restaurants are popping up a little farther south on Highway 50."

"Well, this restaurant is charming. The busboy looks just like the young Englishmen in the framed prints. Blonde hair, rosy cheeks."

Anne laughed.

"Are the hotel rooms done in period pieces as well?"

"Don't know. Never stayed in one." Anne sat up a little straighter, "Oh, good. Our brunch is here. After lunch, we'll stop at the cottage, and then spend the rest of the day in St. Michaels."

Anne opened the door to the cottage and ushered Trish into the main room.

"Oh – Wow. What a gorgeous view." Trish stood in the front room. She walked down the two steps to the sunroom and opened the double doors to the screened porch.

A hundred yards of lawn stretched to Anne's dock and the waters of Swan Cove.

Anne
The Town Dock Restaurant

Later that afternoon, Anne and Trish sank into the Town Dock deck chairs.

Trish rummaged through the shopping bags she'd filled during their expedition along Talbot Street. "It's been a good day. St. Michaels is a great place to go shopping. Thanks for bringing me here."

Anne pointed at the accumulated goods. "You outdid yourself."

A waiter hurried over to their table.

"Hi, Dr. Anne. Good to see you. The usual?"

"Hi, Chance. I'll have my usual Bloody Mary – not too strong, not too spicy."

Anne gestured to her companion. "Chance, this is my friend Trish. We went to Medical School together. She's a pediatrician in Chicago."

"Well, Dr. Trish, I hope you enjoy your time on the Eastern Shore. Will you be staying long?"

"My husband is in Georgetown for a conference. We'll be leaving in a few days." She nodded at Anne, "We'll only be out here for dinner. We're going back to Georgetown tonight. It's been a great day, so far. We did some shopping, and I got to see Anne's cottage."

"You must be thirsty, after all that. Can I get you a drink?"

"A bloody Mary, just like the one Anne ordered. Do you have a good appetizer? I'm too hungry to wait until dinner."

"We have a wonderful crab dip. Will that fill the bill?"

"Yes, please."

Chance turned to Anne. "Stuart and William made reservations for tonight. Are you joining them for dinner?"

Anne smiled and bobbed her head. "Stuart said he reserved a table for four at seven-thirty. I'm sure we'll be sitting inside. It'll be too cool out here when the sun goes down."

"The crab dip will be just right to stave off hunger pangs." Chance hurried off.

"Anne, weren't those men, at the Tidewater Inn today?"

"What men?"

Trish pointed her chin toward two men leaning against the railing. "They came into the dining room at the Inn when we had lunch. And I saw them on Talbot Street. Now they're here."

"St. Michaels is a small town. Not many places to go." She looked a little closer. "That's funny. They were here the last time I had dinner with William and Stuart."

"Here's your drinks, ladies, the crab dip will be out soon."

"Chance, who are those men over by the railing?"

"Don't know, Dr. Anne. I've only seen them once before." He paused and wrinkled his nose. "Don't think they're from around here."

The Followers
April 25, 1989

Arturo and Miguel wandered toward the bar and took the last two stools.

"We need to call in. I'm getting tired of following the damn broad."

Rosie, the bartender, was back on duty. Arturo ordered a Dewar's and water. He tossed some coins to Miguel. "Give the boss a call. Find out if we can get a different assignment."

Miguel shot him a dirty look and huffed. He grabbed the coins, then walked to the payphones.

Minutes later, he returned, his face flushed. "Boss wasn't happy with your request. Said we should follow orders or look for work elsewhere. It looks like we camp out at the post office again. As soon as it gets dark, we're supposed to slash her tires."

"What's the point?"

"The boss doesn't want her to go back to Georgetown. He's sure no one out here's going to have four tires for her car." He shrugged. "He says we should make sure she stays here."

"What the hell?" Miguel's displeasure was obvious.

"Quinlan's back. They're sure he's in DC. The boss thinks Quinlan will show up at her townhouse in the next day or two."

Miguel spat and made a gesture of disgust. "José and Carlos get to make the hit while we're stuck out here? We're the ones who've been going without sleep."

"As soon as it gets dark, we're supposed to take care of her tires."

Anne

Anne looked up and smiled. "Stuart, William. You're early."

"What are you doing outside? It's getting too cool to sit on the deck."

"You're right. Until about five minutes ago, the sun was warm. Do you remember, Trish, my friend from medical school?"

Stuart reached for Trish's hand and all but clicked his heels, "Of course we do. How's the Windy City? Where's your charming husband?"

"Lenny's having dinner with some friends. They're somewhere in Georgetown reminiscing about the 'good ole days.'"

"We're glad to have you two all to ourselves for the evening. I wish you could stay for a few more days. It's Wild Fowl weekend."

Anne laughed. "Oh, that's right. No biggie. Every hunter in the state will be on the Eastern Shore this weekend with his guns and dogs." Anne stood. "Chance is signaling. Our table must be ready."

Trish
The Cottage at Swan Cove

Trish sighed, "Hi, Len, we won't be home tonight. We'll have to stay at the cottage for the night. Somebody slashed Anne's tires." Her friends drove us back to the cottage. The car is still at the restaurant."

"Why would anyone slash Anne's tires?"

"Anne thinks it was some local teenagers with too much time on their hands."

"I'll miss you, Sweetheart."

"I'll miss you, too. What time will your meeting start in the morning?"

"Eight o'clock. I'll have breakfast at the hotel. Maybe I can hook up with some other colleagues."

"Love you. See you tomorrow." Trish hung up the phone.

"Is Lenny upset?" Anne's voice cracked, "I'm sorry we're stuck out here."

Trish forced a light tone. "You've told me often enough how wonderful mornings are at the cottage. Now, I'll find out firsthand. We'll be back in Georgetown tomorrow. Lenny sounded tired. Besides, his meeting starts early tomorrow morning."

"Did you tell him about the black car?"

"No, I didn't want him to worry." Trish looked at Anne, her eyes narrowed. "You don't really think teenagers slashed the tires. You think it was the men who are following you."

Ora
The Next Morning
April 26, 1989

"Captain, Anne never returned to her townhouse last night."

"That doesn't make any sense. I went to Anne's townhouse this morning. When I got there, I saw a guy come out and lock the door. I got in and out pretty quickly. Anne's bed was unmade, and there was lingerie draped across the foot of the bed."

"I got to her place just in time to see you leave this morning. A car with a couple of men had just pulled into a parking space. They were looking for you."

"What makes you think that?"

"As soon as they recognized you, the driver pulled out of the parking space and tried to follow you."

"Why would somebody stay at her place if she wasn't there?"

"Maybe she has friends visiting, Captain. There weren't any men's clothes in the closet, or any other evidence any man spent time there. What time did you get there this morning?"

"About six-fifteen or so. Who's staying at her house?"

Ora shrugged. "I don't know. Anne wasn't at work and wasn't at the house all day yesterday. I didn't hang out here last night."

"Do you think they have her?"

"Don't know. Do you want me to check the cottage?"

"Yes, please. I have a meeting with Agency people this morning. I'll get over to the Eastern Shore as soon as I can."

"Give me a call when you get close. Don't go charging in on your own. I'll have the situation scoped out before you get there. There's an empty lot a little west of her house. You'll see my car. Wait there."

Stuart and William
April 26, 1989

Stuart and William knocked on the cottage door. They carried fresh bagels, berries, half and half, orange juice, and champagne.

"Good Morning, Ladies. Since you're without wheels, we brought breakfast to you."

"Wow! I sure didn't expect this. Thanks, guys. Egg Bagels. My favorite. It's such a beautiful day we should eat on the porch so we can watch the swans. My guess is this will be one of the first nice days this season."

"What time will your car be ready, Anne?"

"The guy at the service station told me he'd call me when it was ready. If I haven't heard from him by noon, I'll call him. They were hoping they could send to Annapolis for the tires. That didn't work. The guys from the service station said they had to purchase them from a pretty far away. I don't know if they're coming from D.C., Dover, or Baltimore. The tires won't be here until late this afternoon."

Connor

There was a nip in the air as Connor got out of the cab. He was several blocks short of his destination.

This weather is a whole lot nicer than the endless summers of Central America. Down there, it's just heat and energy-sapping humidity.

He focused on the business at hand. Knowledge about the meeting would be strictly limited.

Compartmentalization and stringent restrictions on access to information would ensure the leak was traced from its point of origin.

Connor surveyed his surroundings. The street was empty.

It doesn't look like anyone is following me.

Killeen sat at the head of the table. Three other men were already in place, waiting. He breathed a sigh of relief. *Worthington's not here.*

Killeen looked relaxed. "Connor, we're here today to go over what you learned during your trip down south. You remember Stan Korinsky from the Agency and Tony Candura from Defense. Tony's involved in planning the operation in Panama."

Candura must be a colonel by now, maybe even a brigadier general.

Connor knew Korinsky from past operations.

"State won't be joining us. They don't get involved in planning a military operation."

Connor relaxed a bit and smiled. *Donovan got the word to them.*

"Have you met Steve Crowley? He's from the front office. You'll report to him about the information you passed on to Donovan."

Killeen looked around the room. Heads nodded. "Let's get down to business."

No Worthington. Connor gave another small smile and sat a little straighter. *None of these guys will leak information.*

"Connor, please start with your impressions." Killeen gestured to Connor.

"The Panamanian Guardia Nacional will put up a fight against us initially. Not because they support Noriega, just out of national pride," Connor began. "I don't think their opposition to the U.S.

Army will last. The Dignity Battalions will disappear in the face of disciplined American troops. As far as I can tell, Noriega's thugs have little leadership and less initiative."

Connor reported on the business leaders' attitudes and the eventual support any operation would have from the middle and upper classes.

The give and take of the debriefing were mercifully short.

"One thing is clear," Connor paused, "We'll have to make sure a legitimate government is in the wings, ready to succeed Noriega. Our problem is, we can't get the replacement organized beforehand. It'll blow any chance of surprise. If we organize it too late, then we'll have chaos in Panama. The country thrives on business. Take away order and commerce will collapse. If we can't sustain commerce, the social order will crash. Then we'll have to deal with looting and street riots. We don't need another Cuba."

"What do you suggest?" Candura asked. "You want us to have a president waiting in the wings for the next act. Even though we can't tell him what he's waiting for?"

"Exactly. For better or for worse, Guillermo Endara is the duly elected president, even though he never occupied the office. Endara's connection to Interbank is an embarrassment. But he'll have to step up to the presidency when we get rid of Noriega."

Eventually, they developed all the details and came up with a workable plan.

Finally, Killeen put down his pencil and closed his manila file.

Connor remembered one more detail. "There's a perfect landing zone across the street from the Marriott. It's a direct run from the sea and provides quick access to the surrounding area. I took pictures. Donovan has the film."

Killeen, Candura, and Korinsky stood and left the room.

Crowley didn't leave his seat. He finally spoke. "Donovan commands a lot of respect in the Company. He tells me you have a computer disc containing interesting information. Is this true?"

"Have you reviewed it?"

Connor rotated his hand in a so-so gesture. "Not in detail. I think you'll find the names of a lot of bastards who have been laundering drug money." He paused. "I don't think we should go after the people involved in the drug trafficking until we've gotten rid of Noriega."

"I agree - we have to hold off on the drug enforcement action for a while. We can't involve the DEA until the military action is complete." Crowley lifted his coffee mug and slowly sipped his coffee. "Big difference between a major military operation and a drug raid."

Conner nodded, "If the DEA starts questioning or arresting people, it'll tip our hand."

Crowley shrugged. "The information will snowball. The wrong people will know we're coming. We'll wind up with a media storm."

Although Connor understood the logic, he was angry. Noriega, in his downfall, might still win a small victory. "A good man died because he passed the information to me. There are people in our government who profited from the drug trade. It will be up to us to bring them to justice." Every ounce of blood inherited from his Celtic ancestors boiled at the idea that Manuel's death might go un-avenged.

"I'll give Donovan the disc. I give you my word that after the operation, the right people will get the information. I can guarantee a total house cleaning."

Connor pulled the disc from his pocket and slid it across the table. "Unfortunately, someone stole the papers he gave me from my hotel room in Panama."

"I'd like nothing better than to go after these bastards." Crowley frowned. "

Now, I have to figure out how to figure out who the leak is in the State Department."

"You'll find out when you look at the disc."

"All I can promise is the right people in Washington will receive the information. That's the extent of what I can do."

Crowley picked up the disc and walked to a Diebold file cabinet. It was as secure as any safe. "We have to stay focused."

Connor walked from the brownstone. He pulled up the collar of his trench coat and smiled.

Paul Garcia
The Same Day

Paul Garcia was the Assistant United States Attorney for the Southern District of New York. His current task was to lead the ongoing anti-drug investigation. His fluency in Spanish was a great asset, and his ability to manage the team working for him was an attribute.

Paul studied a report that had just come across his desk when his phone buzzed. "A Doctor Neff is here to see you. She said you're not expecting her, but she has something for you from Connor Quinlan."

"Send her in, please."

Garcia suspected his old classmate was involved in undercover work. Connor had too many unexplained absences and unusual travel patterns. Paul wondered how Elke Neff was involved with Connor. Was she a friend? A clandestine associate? A lover? She was too good looking for the former and too smart for it to be the latter.

The gorgeous blond walked into his office.

Garcia was pleased to see the beautiful blond woman. He smiled as she walked through the door.

"Elke, I'm glad to see you. My office is pretty far from your hunting grounds. What brings you here today? Would you like a cup of coffee?"

"No, but thanks. I'm just a delivery girl today. I can only stay for a minute. Way too much work waiting for me at the office." She reached into her handbag, pulled out the computer disc, and slid it across Paul's desk. "Connor left this at my place and asked me to get it to you."

She turned to leave.

"Wait. How's Connor? What's he up to? I know he must be working on some weird case."

"Don't know. Connor finds me. He's always exhausted and hungry when I hear from him. All I do is pick him up, patch him up, perk him up, and pack him off. He said the disc was important and asked me to make sure you got it. Paul took the CD without taking his eyes off Elke. Not sure of how much of her story he could

168   G l o r i a   C a s a l e

believe. "Thanks. If you talk to Connor, give him my regards. Tell him I'd like to have dinner with him soon."

She grinned. "I get first dibs on a dinner with Connor." She tossed her head and was out the door before he had a chance to respond.

Garcia stared at the disc.

What could be so important?

He slipped the disc into his computer.

There were lists of bank accounts. Each had enormous amounts of money in them.

Most of the names on the accounts were false.

Winston Churchill? I don't think he's with us anymore. Hemmingway? I don't think he's around either. Then there's a bunch of numbered accounts.

Garcia dialed an associate, "Sam, can you come to my office right away? I need your help."

Sam Feldman

Sam Feldman, an unlikely FBI agent, was the resident computer geek in Garcia's office, a CPA who worked on Garcia's team for two years at the State Department. He could recognize false entries in accounts and sense irregularities.

Garcia often said Sam could put more bad guys away with his index finger and a computer keyboard than any other agent could with a gun.

He punched in Feldman's extension number. "Hey, Sam. Can you come to my office? We've got a situation."

Feldman arrived to find Garcia staring at his computer screen. "Did you screw up your computer again?"

Garcia shook his head and gestured to a chair. "Come around to this side of the desk. Check this out."

Feldman sat next to the boss, stared at the screen, and scrunched his forehead. "Looks like accounts from various banks. What's with the fake names?"

"A lot of money's being transferred from account to account." He split the screen and had two pages side by side. "Look here – a withdrawal from this account," Sam pointed to a transaction, "coincides with this deposit." He tapped a set of figures on the right page. "Looks like classic money laundering."

Feldman slid over, "Lemme play with it." He quickly became entranced by the screen.

"Ho-l-y shit!" Feldman's exclamation startled Paul.

"That was quick. What'd you find?

"The Mother Lode. Did you see the supplement at the end of this thing?"

Paul shook his head. "I knew it was way out of my expertise when I opened the file."

"The accounts have an index correlating the names and numbers on the accounts to actual names." Sam blinked. "Y' gotta see this. Money goes from Columbia to Washington, DC, then to Switzerland, to California, then to New York, and finally, back to DC."

"Test the information on the disc. See if it's real. I got the disc from a reliable source. I'm guessing it will check out."

Fred Worthington

Fred, unable to gather information about Connor, slammed his hand on the desk. Desperation replaced his smug attitude.

Quinlan's back in town. His stomach cramped. *And, they didn't call me for the debriefing.*

He pushed away from his desk and stretched. There was no relief in the tension in his back.

"Damn." *I wasted two hundred dollars on lunch yesterday. Korinsky didn't give me a clue.*

Sweat trickled down Fred's back. *Every time I brought up Quinlan's name, Korinsky told me another amusing story. Quinlan in South America. Quinlan in Iraq. Quinlan here, Quinlan there, Quinlan everywhere but Panama.*

He stared at the phone, willing it to ring.

A feeling of dread squeezed his gut.

Fred pulled out an already damp handkerchief. He knew the drug lords could dispose of him. A fresh patina of sweat covered his brow. *They'd take me down in the blink of an eye.*

He drummed his fingers on his desk.

He waited for a return phone call from a friend involved with a company doing business between Florida and Panama. *I shared some inside information to help him out last year.*

Fred was sure his friend must have heard something about Quinlan's trip to Panama.

The private line rang. Fred had a moment of hope.

He looked at his watch. Sweat ran down his back.

"Hello?" his voice was tentative.

"Señor Worthington." The familiar Hispanic growl greeted him. "It's been an hour. Why haven't we heard from you?"

"I h-haven't been able to find Quinlan. His trip to Panama was only to meet with business associates. There was no clandestine activity planned."

"You fool," Estrada lost his calm and shouted, "A chambermaid has more sense than you. She made a few dollars by being nosey and making sure her neighborhood captain got the information. Noriega gave me papers from Quinlan's hotel room. El Hombre knows Quinlan's visit went far beyond an exchange of port information."

Worthington shook. His breathing and his speech became increasingly rapid.

"I can't find him. I've tried. They excluded me from the debriefing. No one will give me any information."

"They suspect you. How inconvenient for you. I have men in Washington. Good men, but they're not magicians. They're getting impatient, and so am I. Colonel Noriega shares my concern. Mr. Quinlan has information. Too much information. Do you think I would call you for anything less?"

"But ..." The line was dead.

Fred was short of breath. His chest ached.

His fingers were numb. *I feel like I'm having a heart attack.* The pain in his chest was persistent.

When Fred agreed to this pact with the devil, he hadn't considered the downside. All he saw was the money, the country club, big house, beautiful cars, and expensive clothes for his wife and the pretty little woman he kept on the side. It sounded so good. It seemed so easy.

He knew the good life would be over as soon as the word got out.

The clubs would cancel his membership. Judith would divorce him. His mistress would lock him out of her life. He shivered. His kids would have to leave the Capitol Hill Day School.

NSA

The NSA computers were programmed to look for certain pre-determined 'trigger words.' These words would excite their interest and prompt them to start recording.

The amount of information the computer could collect was overwhelming.

This morning one of the computers at Ft. Mead began to record an international call.

The conversation would be reviewed much later by an analyst.

The analyst, tasked to look for information from or about Panama, would listen to the recordings and decide its relevance.

For now, the computer snatched and held tight to the secret. It would take several days for people at NSA to review the tape.

Connor
The Same Day

Connor crossed M Street and headed for the C & O canal. His pager vibrated as he turned on to the footpath along the canal. He checked the message. *Ora.* Connor looked around to find a phone booth.

Ora answered halfway through the first ring. "Captain, things don't look good. I'm in St. Michaels. Someone slashed Anne's tires last night."

"Slashed?"

"They slashed all four tires. Anne's car is in the repair shop. I'm willing to bet the two thugs who've been watching her did it."

"Stay there. It sounds like an attempt to set a trap for me. I'll be over as soon as I can get a car."

"A little past Anne's place, there's an overgrown field. A lot of brush and cover. I have my car parked next to a boathouse. Meet me there."

Connor took the Metro to Washington National Airport.

So far, so good. Wonder how much longer my luck will hold.

He used an alternate identity to rent a nondescript blue Ford sedan. Within a half-hour, he was on his way to the Eastern Shore. His anxiety increased as he drove over the Bay Bridge and headed for the Tidewater Inn.

The Inn, established in 1712, started as a wooden guesthouse. The current brick building was completed in 1944 and combined the ambiance of colonial Maryland with the conveniences of a luxury hotel.

Connor signed in with the same identity he'd used to lease the vehicle. His room was clean and bright, but it looked as if it hadn't been altered anytime in the last century. All the furniture pieces were eighteenth-century reproductions. It felt like walking backward in time.

George Washington would have been comfortable in this room.

Twenty minutes later, Connor turned onto the overgrown road to the boathouse.

Ora stepped out of the shadow of the building.

Connor tilted his head toward the passenger seat and leaned over to unlock the door. Ora slid into the car. Connor drove to the center of St. Michaels.

The high-backed booths at the Talbot Street Tavern provided a bit of privacy as well as charm.

Connor picked up the menu. "Bring me up to date."

"Did you check out the sedan in the Newcomb post office parking lot?"

The waitress arrived at the table.

"One of your fabulous hamburgers, please," Connor handed the menu to the young woman. "And a cup of coffee."

"Same for me," Ora added.

Connor and Ora waited while the waitress fussed with napkins and silverware.

When the waitress left, Ora continued, "The men in the car have been watching Anne for days. They're the ones I told you about. They were on her in Georgetown and followed her to the cottage yesterday."

"You said they have a second team at her house now."

Ora nodded. "They do. I think someone's covering all the bases looking for you."

Connor gave a wry smile and a nod. "They're hoping to trap me."

"Is Anne alone?"

"No, a friend is with her."

"A guy?" Connor crumpled his napkin and threw it on the table.

"No, a woman – a woman about her age. I think she's visiting from out of town. I'm pretty sure the guy at the townhouse is the woman's husband."

A wave of hope swept over Connor. *Why would they be sleeping in her bedroom?* He cleared his throat. "What else?"

"They still haven't fixed her tires. This morning, our old friends from Bogotá showed up with bags of food. When I left, Anne, her friend, and our old friends were all sitting on the porch, drinking coffee – watching the swans float by."

The waitress plopped down the plates of food and coffee. "Anything else?"

"No, thanks," the men chorused.

Connor picked up his hamburger with both hands. "I'm surprised they haven't figured out you're around."

"They're amateurs. They leave their cigarette butts all around the car when they park it by the post office. They sit in the car like dummies and stare at Anne's driveway. And, they haven't even attempted to look like the locals."

Anne

Anne hung up the phone. She turned to her guests. "That was the service station." She heaved a sigh. "Carl said the tires are at a place in *Dover*. He won't get them until this afternoon."

Trish shrugged her shoulders and smiled. "Can we get in another day of shopping?"

"Don't you want to stay on the porch and watch the swans?"

The look Trish gave her was answer enough.

"Lenny would love the print we saw at the frame shop. I'll bet they can make arrangements to send it to Illinois. And, I saw a few things I'd want to pick up for my sisters. And I want to check out the clothes in that little boutique. I'm still salivating. I could use something stunning for the upcoming festivities."

Anne turned to Stuart. "Would you mind if we hitch a ride back to St. Michaels with you?"

"No problem at all. You'll be able to walk to Carl's shop to get your car later. He should have it fixed by the time you're finished shopping."

"Good idea. We'll be ready in a few minutes. As soon as I wash the dishes." Anne piled the dishes in the sink, squirted the detergent on them, and turned on the hot water. "Trish, what's Lenny's schedule for today?"

"He'll be tied up in meetings until early evening. We have lots of time."

A few hours later, Anne piled the bags Trish had accumulated during their shopping spree in the trunk of her car. "Looks like you cleaned out most of the stores in St. Michaels. And, we never even got to the Christmas Shop."

"Better skip it this trip. As it is, Lenny'll have a royal fit cramming all this stuff in our suitcases."

Anne began to giggle.

Her mirth was contagious.

The women couldn't stop laughing.

Finally, Anne caught her breath. "Let's stop at the cottage. The dishes will be dry. I'll put them away. Then we can head back to town."

Trish checked her wristwatch. "We'll get back in time to have dinner with Len."

"Sound's good. Let's see. Where would you like to go for dinner? Should I call Ruth Chris' Steakhouse and make a reservation?"

"Sounds good to me. It's a shame Lenny doesn't have a way to come out here. He'd love a Maryland crab dinner."

"I could call Jimmy's Seafood Restaurant in Dundalk. It's a bit of a drive from Georgetown – but we'd be in crab heaven."

Anne slid the last dish into the cupboard. "That takes care of everything here. Can't think of anything else. Time to head back to Georgetown."

Trish picked up the bag of groceries Anne wanted to take back to Georgetown. "I'm ready."

"Did you decide where you want to have dinner? If we want dinner reservations, I should make them before we leave. Ruth Chris or Jimmy's?"

"Whatever you think."

"Jimmy's it is."

Trish looked out at the cove. "I'm almost sorry we have to leave. It's *so* quiet and peaceful out here. The thought of going back to the noise of Chicago is depressing."

"That's funny…" Anne jiggled the phone receiver.

Trish looked away from the lake. "What?"

"The phone's dead."

Trish looked up. "Anne, we've got company," Her voice held a tinge of panic.

A man stormed into the house. "Sit down - both of you. Don't move." He gestured toward Anne with a revolver. "Come in, Arturo," he shouted.

There was a muffled response. "The screen doors are locked. I can't get on the porch."

"Come around to the front door. We're in no hurry." He waved the weapon again. "Sit down. Both of you."

The women complied.

He grinned at Anne. "Let's see how long it takes your boyfriend to get here."

Connor

Connor opened the back gate to Stuart and William's yard. Stuart's convertible and William's SUV were in their usual places. "Anybody home?"

"What a surprise." Stuart stepped from behind a holly tree. "I thought you were off on some mission." He placed clippers on a bench, brushed the soil off his hands, and walked, hand extended, toward Connor.

"Just got back. I just happened to be in the area. Thought I'd stop in to see you."

Stuart frowned. "You just *happened* to be in St. Michaels?"

"You haven't changed a bit. Suspicious as ever."

Stuart opened the back door and ushered Connor inside. "With good reason. Let me call William. He's upstairs in the study. We've been trying to figure out how to get in touch with *you*. I even called your office about a week ago."

Connor grimaced. He never read the list of calls Angela handed him before he left the office.

"I haven't returned any calls in the past week. The Company had a small problem that required my immediate attention." He laughed. I came out here to check on a few things. I'll stop at the cottage to see Anne on my way back to the office."

"Anne said they would be going back to Georgetown about an hour ago."

Connor sighed, "I was going to stop to see her on my way out of town."

William entered the kitchen. "Good to see you. It's been a while. Take a seat. We'll fill you in what's been happening and what has us concerned."

Stuart set the table. "How do you like the tea-set? It's from the SS United States. We bought it at auction a few years ago."

Connor smiled. "You two are still collecting." He paused. "My Uncle Harry was into classic ocean liners. I'll see if there are any of his pictures in my attic. He left most of his collection to me. I haven't had a chance to go through it all."

Stuart pointed to the table.

Connor sat.

Stuart poured his tea. "Why did you call last week?"

"Anne, of course. There have been some strange things happening. We wanted to make sure you knew about them. We considered a call to headquarters. We were afraid it might have something to do with your recent travels."

"You were worried about Anne? Get on with it."

" We're concerned. Anne might be in some kind of danger."

"Define danger."

"About two weeks ago, someone broke into her cottage. Anne met us at the Town Dock for dinner that night. She didn't say anything about expecting a visitor. Whoever it was, showed up in the middle of the Nor'easter we had that night. He pulled the screen door off its hinges and did some damage to the inside of the house. We noticed bruises on her arms the next day."

"Did you confront her about any of this?"

"Sort of – she told us the storm caused the damage to the house. We knew that didn't make any sense. She never mentioned the bruises."

Ora only reported the damage to the cottage. "Tell me more."

"Anne tried to hide the bruises with makeup – but they looked like fingerprints."

Connor looked from Stuart to William. "Fingerprints? What else?"

"We had dinner with Anne last night." Stuart shrugged. "Anne and a woman she went to medical school with came out to do some shopping. We met them at the Town Dock for dinner. While we were eating dinner, someone slashed her tires."

"Any clues about who did it?"

"Not really. There have been some tough-looking guys in St. Michaels recently. They only show up when Anne's here. Come to think of it – I don't remember seeing them at the Town Dock last night."

"Do you think they're responsible?"

She doesn't recognize them. And, they're not locals."

"Were they the ones who broke into the cottage and caused the damage?"

"No. Anne must know the person who attacked her. And, she must have a good reason for not reporting the attack."

"You've got a point." Connor gave a quick nod. "Keep me posted about anything of concern. I'll tell Angela to put you on the priority list."

"Thanks. It sounds like you're going back to New York."

"I'm planning on it. How was your dinner with Anne?"

"Wonderful. Anne and her friend, Trish, spent yesterday afternoon shopping in St. Michaels. From the pile of bags, they packed into Anne's car, it looked like they had a good time. We enjoyed dinner. It would have been even better if Trish's husband could have joined us. He stayed at Anne's townhouse last night."

"Why didn't he come out?"

"Trish and her husband are both doctors. Trish and Anne were in the same Medical School Class. The classmate's husband was in Georgetown to attend a medical conference. He planned on having dinner with friends."

It must have been their stuff in Anne's bedroom. "Then what happened?"

"When we walked them to the car, the tires on Anne's car were flat."

William put down his teacup. "Carl towed the car over to his shop. And, we drove Anne and Trish back to the cottage."

"Was that a good idea?"

"We didn't think so. We tried to talk the women into staying with us. But they were determined to spend the night at the cottage."

"Did you call them this morning?"

"Even better than that. We brought bagels and mimosas to their house. We stayed for breakfast. Then drove them back to town to do more shopping. Carl expected the replacement tires around noon. Last I heard, they were hoping to get back to Georgetown in time for dinner."

"Does Anne know someone's following her?

Stuart shrugged his shoulders. "I'm not sure."

"What do you mean?"

"She asked us about the men. She noticed them at the Town Dock and reminded us that they insisted on sitting at a table close to us last week."

"Are you sure they're not locals?"

"Definitely not locals." Stuart's reply was emphatic.

William nodded in agreement. "One of them left the restaurant twice last night. His second absence took a long time. I'm sure he was the one who slashed Anne's tires."

Connor's pager vibrated. He checked the number. "Can I use your phone?"

"Of course. It's in the TV room. If you need some privacy, you can use the one in the upstairs study."

Ora answered on the first ring. "Captain, we have a situation. Those guys from the car in the post office parking lot are holding Anne and her friend captive in the cottage."

"Captive?"

"They're holding them at gunpoint."

"Keep watching. I'll be there as quick as I can."

Connor walked back into the dining room. "Gotta go. Thanks for the tea."

William frowned.

"Trouble?"

"Yes." Connor walked toward the door. "Thanks for the tea and cake."

He drove into the center of St. Michaels. *Thank goodness, the general store hasn't closed yet.* He glanced at the sky. *Better get moving. Full dark will make things more difficult.*

He bought a black sweatshirt and a penlight.

A few minutes later, he parked his car behind the boathouse. Ora appeared from the shadows.

How is he able to maintain his invisibility? He's so big. But he can move like a cat.

Ora pointed to Anne's cottage. "Two men are in the house with Anne and another woman. They're the same guys who've been following her. I've been able to get up close to the house. Things are quiet."

"You said the men were armed. If they haven't hurt anyone, I'm guessing they're waiting for me. Are you up to a little action?"

Ora smiled and nodded. "I've been away from any kind of real action for far too long." He grinned. "Can't wait."

The two men crossed the field. They stayed in the shadows and moved toward the cottage. They reverted to habits they had formed years ago.

Connor gestured to Ora. "You take the front. I'll go around back. He edged along the side of the building.

Several loops of wire and an old rake handle poked out from an opening between the cottage pilings.

A smile played across Connor's lips.

He made a wire loop and laid it on the next to the last step, then strung the wire to the corner of the porch.

He entered the small shed attached to the cottage and opened the power box, pulled the main switch, waited for a second, and then turned it back on. He repeated the maneuver about a minute later. The third time he didn't turn the power back on.

Connor crouched near the porch, shielded by a small bush growing near the stairs.

The Watchers

The lights went off, leaving the cottage in complete darkness. The sudden black-out startled the two men. They flashed off and on again.

By the third time, the men were near panic.

"Where's your electric box?" Arturo snarled. He jammed his revolver under Anne's chin, then rattled off something in Spanish to Ricardo.

"At the back of the house, on the left-hand side." Anne pointed in the general direction of the box.

"You better not be lying." Arturo gestured to his companion. "Get out there."

Ricardo went to the back door, looked out, and hesitated. He would have to grope his way through the dark. Another string of Spanish curses from Arturo galvanized Ricardo into action. He shoved his gun in his belt and unhooked the screen door.

A wooden staircase led from the porch to the grassy yard.

The stair rails were slick with dew. Ricardo grasped the rails and slowly descended.

When he planted his foot on the last step, Connor yanked the wire tight around Ricardo's left ankle. He fell forward. A blow to the back of his neck silenced him before he could shout a warning or reach for his weapon.

Arturo paced inside the cottage. He went to the back door and peered into the darkness. "Get in here, Ricardo. Where the hell are you?"

No answer.

"Damn," he mumbled and slammed the door.

"Maybe Ricardo fell." Anne prodded. "He may be injured."

The instructions the boss gave Arturo were simple. Capture Quinlan. Do not kill him. *We're only supposed to hold the doctora to make Quinlan come out of hiding.*

"Maybe he can't find the box." Anne patted Trish's hand. "It's okay," she whispered to her friend.

"You want me to go out there so you can run out the front door. You must think I'm stupid."

"He could be injured," Anne insisted, "If he's okay, he'd be back by now."

Arturo looked out the back door again. If he went outside, the two women wouldn't be in his line of sight. He walked to the front door, opened it, and waved the gun back and forth. If either of you run, I'll shoot you."

Both women stayed frozen in place.

He flicked on the exterior light a few times and found it wasn't working.

"Ricardo?" Another string of Spanish.

Arturo took one step down the brick stairs. Someone knocked his knees out from under him and ripped the gun from his grasp. A large hand tightened around his neck.

Arturo's thoughts became jumbled and confused.

Ora

Ora jammed the gun against the man's right temple. "If you move or make a sound, I will be happy to kill you." Ora snarled, "Comprendez?"

Arturo nodded.

Ora pulled Arturo to his feet and pushed him to the side of the cottage where Connor was waiting.

"We lucked out. Not a lot of smarts between them. Tie him up. Throw him in the shed, next to the other one." Connor pointed to the small wooden addition. There's some rope hanging from a hook inside.

Arturo, bound and gagged was laid him next to Ricardo on the dirt floor of the shed.

Connor

Connor turned the electricity on and walked in the front door of the cottage.

Anne ran to him. "Are you all right?"

He held her tight. "I'm fine." He held her at arm's length. "Looks like you're okay." He smiled. "Those guys are tied up. I'm sorry this happened. They were after me, not you."

"They said they were waiting for you. I'm so glad to see you. I was worried about you." Tears filled her eyes.

Looking over Anne's shoulder, Connor saw Trish sitting on the day bed. She stared wide-eyed at some distant nothing.

"Hi, remember me?" He waved and smiled. "Hi, Trish, It's me – Connor. We met several years ago."

Trish could only nod.

Ora laughed, "How about an introduction, Captain."

Anne jumped at the sound of Ora's voice. Her eyes went wide. "Oh my god, where did you come from?"

"Ora's been watching over you for the past few days."

"Watching over me? Why would someone watch over me?"

"I was sure you were in danger. Do you have Stuart's phone number?"

"His number is on the list by the phone. Please tell me what's going on." She looked back at Ora. "Are you the big goon?"

Ora shrugged. "What big goon?"

"It's a long story."

Connor picked up the receiver. "No dial tone."

"Maybe they cut the phone line,"

Connor pointed his chin at Ora. "Check the phone line."

Anne reached for her flashlight. "You'll need this. There's electrical tape in the top right-hand drawer in the kitchen."

Ora returned minutes later. "You were right. They cut the wire. I spliced it together. The phone should work now."

Connor dialed the number. Before the second ring, he heard a familiar voice. "William, this is Connor. I'm at Anne's cottage. Need some help."

"You're at Anne's? I thought she left for Georgetown hours ago. Is she okay?"

"She's fine. I'll explain when you get here. Do you know anyone on the local police who can be discreet? I need to make arrangements to have some strangers picked up."

"One of the local cops is a retired MP. He's a friend. I'll call him. We'll be there in a few minutes."

Before he hung up, Connor heard William shout. "Stuart, put your shoes on."

Connor smiled. *They never seem to change.*

In less than fifteen minutes, William and Stuart walked in, followed by a uniformed police officer. No flashing lights.

Ora stood silent against the wall.

William looked across the room and took a step backward. "Stuart. Look who's here." He pointed at Ora, then he turned and quietly whispered to Anne. "He's always scared me a little."

Anne paced the few steps across the living room and back. She turned to Connor. "You knew Stuart and William in the past?" Her voice was accusing and carried a hit of hurt. "Why didn't you tell me? How do you know them?"

Connor led her to a chair. "I've known William and Stuart for many years. Once upon a long time ago, we were all in a similar line of business."

She pointed toward the back of the cottage. "Who sent them?"

"The people who employ the two men out in the shed were using you to get me. Right now, I don't know how their bosses made the connection between us. Those guys are nothing more than hired help."

Stuart interrupted, "Connor, meet Sergeant Steve Moeller, retired military police. He's another smart one who decided to spend his declining years in Saint Michaels.

Connor shook hands with Moeller. "Sergeant, could you secure a couple of prisoners until the feds pick them up? We'd appreciate discretion and no paperwork."

"Yes, Sir. William explained it to me. I'll take care of it. When'll someone be here to collect them?"

Connor dialed another number. "Donovan, I'm in Newcomb. Got a situation going on out here. A couple of thugs were holding Anne and a friend captive. They tried to set a trap for me. We need a clean-up crew to pick them up. I'll tell you the rest when I see you."

Donovan's deep voice resonated. "I'll get someone out there to pick up the trash. They'll have to come over from Ft. Mead." Donovan paused. "I am not pleased. Someone was trying to capture you, AND they used a civilian to set the trap. We'll get every bit of information out of them. I'll see to it." Another brief silence. "By the way, I spoke to the FBI right after I saw you in Washington. They're ready to take care of the domestic investigation. Get back here. You need to be debriefed."

"All kinds of good news." Connor hung up the phone and turned to William. "I have to get to Washington as soon as possible. Can you two stay here with Anne until relief gets here? Should take them about an hour to get here."

"We'll be here," Stuart assured him.

William grinned, "I'm guessing you can't tell us anything about that either."

Connor's rueful smile echoed his answer, "Some things never change."

William turned toward the tall policeman. "Steve, you better check those guys. Stuart will go with you."

Connor turned and hugged Anne. "I'll be back as soon as I can." He motioned to Ora.

The gravel on the small road leading to the cottage crunched as they walked toward the main road. Ora pointed to a car parked in the shadow of a tree. "I have to get to Langley. People are waiting for me. It was good serving with you again, Captain." Their handclasp was strong.

"Thanks for your help."

"Good luck to you, Sir. You'll need it. That lady's got guts."

Connor saluted Ora's departing vehicle. Then turned and walked toward his car. He paused and glanced toward the cottage. *Anne needs me.*

Connor shook his head. "Damn it." He turned and walked back to the cottage.

Anne

Anne walked Connor to his vehicle. He held her close and kissed her forehead and her neck—one long, lingering kiss before he smoothed her hair back.

I have to go back to Washington to make my report. They weren't happy to even give me one day's grace. I'm glad I was here – now."

Anne watched his car weave it's way to the highway.

Anne's emotions were in overdrive. She'd been made a hostage. William and Stuart were not what they seemed. A huge man named Ora had been following her. And, now, Connor was gone, again.

Trish sat next to Anne on the day bed. Her hands shook. "Is everything okay now? Are we safe?"

Anne nodded. "Yes, thanks to Connor and his friend."

"THAT was your Connor?"

Anne bobbed her head.

A wave of amazement washed across Trish's face.

Fred Worthington

Fred sat at the bar in the country club. He was about halfway through a very dry martini.

The bartender handed him the phone. "Call for you, Fred."

A few minutes later, Fred speed-walked to his car.

The damn Cartel is watching me.

He stopped and looked around. The greens-keepers were busy were at a distant green. A gardener was busy cutting daffodils back. He didn't look up as Fred walked by.

"How the hell do they expect me to find Quinlan?" he shouted to no-one.

Fred slid into the driver's seat and covered his face with his hands. He sobbed.

I've called the entire team. Everyone denies hearing from Quinlan.

Connor

Connor headed north on Route 50 toward the Chesapeake Bay Bridge. When he reached Wye Mills, he saw two cars speeding south on Route 50. *That must be the Ft. Meade team.*

At Kent Narrows, he stopped, picked up a container of coffee, and made a call. "Killeen, I'm coming in. I'll be at the office in about forty-five minutes." He hung up without waiting for an acknowledgment.

Thirty minutes later, Connor walked toward Killeen's office. Except for a lone dog walker, the neighborhood was quiet.

Killeen opened the door as soon as Connor leaned on the bell. He motioned Connor into the building. "You look like crap. Get a cup of coffee and tell me what's going on."

Connor slumped into a chair.

Donovan waited in a comfortable chair across the room.

Connor ran his fingers through his hair. "Two thugs were staked out at Anne's cottage over in Newcomb. It's a long story. I didn't try to interrogate them." He pointed to Donovan. "Figured it was up to his Donovan's to get the information."

Donovan refilled his coffee cup. "Sounds like hired goons working for one of the Cartels. I'm guessing they staked out the doctor's place to try to capture you."

Connor walked over to the Mister Coffee machine and poured himself a cup. "Yeah, but how did they connect Anne to me? And how did they know I was in Panama. I didn't tell Anne or anyone else where I was going."

Donovan raised his eyebrows and shoulders, "Whoever's providing the information must be in our loop. Someone who's read into the project. Noriega doesn't have clandestine operatives here."

Connor shrugged. "Before they captured Manuel D'Ormando, he gave me a fair amount of information about the flow of drug money."

"A lot of things have happened since you returned from Panama. You've been out of touch. The FBI office in New York got some information. The State Department is investigating one of their own. But of course, you wouldn't know anything about those events."

Killeen's sarcasm was evident. "Seems like your friend, Paul Garcia, works for the FBI."

"Paul and I were in law school together. He's a damn good agent. He must have happened on something."

Donovan's eyebrows went up. "Happened on something? *My ass.* Somehow, you got information to Garcia about drug dealing and money laundering in Panama. The whole thing has fallen right on the seam of domestic investigation and international intelligence. I don't need a turf war. Justice took the lead in this investigation. There must be a trail that leads to someone who was in the loop. Someone who knew you were going to Panama."

Connor sat back and smiled. *I knew Paul would be all over this one.* "The focus should be on Panama. Get the people together. I'll fill everyone in."

"We 're pulling the meeting together. Get some rest. I'll call you when we're ready."

Connor
April 26, 1989

Three hours later, a young woman tapped Connor's shoulder. "Mr. Quinlan?"

Connor sat bolt upright. Early morning sunlight filtered through the blinds.

"The meeting will start in a few minutes."

He looked at his watch.

On his way to the conference room, Connor picked up a phone in one of the vacant offices. Angela answered on the second ring.

"Mr. Quinlan's office."

"Hi, Angela. Any messages?"

"Nice of you to call in once in a while. Should I bother to ask what you're doing and when you'll be back?"

"No, you shouldn't ask, and I have no idea when I'll be back."

"An Isobel Duarte called. She's at the Saint Regis Hotel. Says she has some information. Paul Garcia called. He wouldn't leave a message."

"I'll call Garcia and Isobel Duarte later. Gotta run."

Connor smiled. Some days he was sure he had nothing to do with running his office.

Killeen sat at the head of the table. Steve Crowley, Stan Korinsky from the DIA, and Tony Candura from Defense stopped their conversation when Connor entered. A fifth person Connor didn't know was at the table. Donovan eased into an armchair near the coffee pot.

Killeen gestured toward the new man. "Connor, this is Walt Peters. He was part of the team from NSA."

"Glad to meet you. I assume you're getting a lot of intercepts."

Killeen nodded and opened a file in front of him. "Mr. Peters group has been monitoring pirate broadcasts from Panama."

Connor smiled, "I've heard about the guy broadcasting opposition to Noriega. Word is he was driving Noriega nuts."

"Do you know who it is?" Peters had his pen poised. "He's not one of ours."

"Kurt Muse."

"Far as we know, he's been doing this on his own," Peters added.

"Kurt's a good guy with a-lotta guts. We should do anything and everything to protect him," Donovan muttered from his corner of the room.

A vigorous nod from Peters, "Independence isn't the safest characteristic when you're taking on a despot. Especially one like Noriega."

"The locals are sure Muse is in Carcel Modella. It's a wonder he's not dead already."

"My friends in Panama were sure they would capture and kill Muse. I'd be surprised if he's not dead already."

Donovan looked over toward Killeen.

"Muse is still alive. We'll extract him before we move in with a major offensive."

Donovan stood, "At our last meeting, I said we'd have to put off involvement with the drug issue. There's an informant inside our government. We'll have to deal with him before we can move forward. Otherwise, he'll jeopardize our operations. The FBI's taking care of the informant."

Connor, still uneasy about how far he could go without endangering his sources, stared back. *Manuel lost his life protecting me. They used Anne.*

Donovan pulled Manuel's computer disc from the Diebold safe. He tapped the envelope on his wrist. "This disc must have some interesting information on it. The FBI seems to have a copy of the data. Do you know anything about how they got the information?"

Connor shrugged and smiled, "I didn't hand it over to them. I told you my suspicions about the contents. As I remember, you weren't interested in the information."

"Touché," Donovan growled. "I was wrong." He pointed toward the foot of the table. "The floor is yours. I hope you have some information for us."

Connor reported what he learned in Panama. He omitted Isobel's information. "I've received affirmation of Connor's report. Shipping and banking industries are being used to move drugs and launder money.

Killeen's phone buzzed. "Please, show them to my office." He shoved his papers into a manila folder. "Our friends from the FBI are here," he announced to the room in general.

Paul Garcia and Sam Feldman entered the room. Donovan shook hands with Garcia. "No need to be formal. He introduced the men sitting at the table. I think you already know Connor Quinlan."

Paul Garcia smiled. "Connor and I are old friends." He shook Connor's hand. "Good to see you." Paul nodded to the man with him, "Sam Feldman is an expert at tracking finances and peeling back information on money laundering setups."

Sam gave a quick nod to the men at the table and opened his file. "Paul asked me to come today because of one of the names I discovered in the data." Sam paused, "a person from the State Department."

Donovan interrupted. "I made sure our contact at State was isolated from any information regarding Connor's whereabouts. Until we're satisfied this is under control, he won't get any information."

He turned to Peters. "Walt, fill us in on what your team found."

"We intercepted phone conversations from Panama and Columbia to someone at State." Walt's voice was shaky and hesitant. "My team recorded transcripts of those conversations." He paused and swiped at his brow with a handkerchief.

Until today, Walt Peters remained insulated from clandestine operations.

"Give us a brief account of the team's report," Donovan's voice was low. Quiet.

Walt gulped, "Someone in Latin America was leaning on a person in Washington for information about Mr. Quinlan."

"Information?"

"Classified information. An unusual level of interest."

Fred Worthington
April 29, 1989

Fred arrived at his State Department office at twelve forty-five. His head ached.

I drank too much champagne at the reception last night.

As he approached his secretary's desk, she stood. "You can't go in there." She pointed toward his office door.

"What are you talking about? Why not?"

"Some men were here working on your computer. They locked your office and told me not to allow anyone to enter. Not even you. There's a vacant office up the hall. I'm pretty sure there's a computer in there.

"Did the technicians say what's wrong?" Fred mustered with as much composure as he could. Rivulets of sweat snaked down his spine.

"All they told me was to make sure *no one* went into the office."

Worthington booted up the computer in the vacant office. The system denied him access.

He tried a second time. A screen opened. Contact Your System Administrator in red letters framed in white against a black screen blinked, once, twice, three times.

Fred opened the door and peeked down the hall. He watched the door to his office close behind a man wearing a dark suit.

The hair on the back of Fred's neck went up. *Agents.* He fought down nausea, crept from the office and strolled toward the far stairwell

Stay calm. Don't draw attention. Look like any employee walking down the hall.

He closed his eyes and bit his lip to keep from running.

When the hall door closed behind him, Fred took the stairs two at a time. He was panting by the time he reached the ground floor. Fred headed for the main exit.

Fred slid into his car and drove home as fast as he could. He breathed a sigh of relief. The circular driveway in front of his house was clear.

He shouted hello as he closed the entry door. No one answered.

Penny's not here. The maid must be shopping.

Fred bolted up the wide stairs to his study and breathed a sigh of relief. *Nothing looks disturbed.* The file cabinet was still locked.

They haven't been here yet.

Fred dialed the combination, pulled out an unlabeled file, took out his Smith and Wesson .38 caliber revolver, and put it into his briefcase

Fred drove aimlessly. He repeatedly checked his rear-view mirror.

Maybe I could leave the country. Fred headed toward BWI.

He pulled out his wallet. Lots of credit cards. Very little cash.

Maybe I can get some money from an ATM. "SHIT," the strangled scream echoed off the car windows. *They've probably sealed my accounts and alerted the airports.*

A flare of hope – I'll call my lawyer. The idea floated around his consciousness for a full minute. Then Fred started laughing. *The cartel would chew him up and flush him down the toilet.*

Fred's bowels cramped. Tears rolled down his cheeks.

He pulled off the highway and buried his face in his hands.

The Columbians?

A burst of uncontrolled laughter.

As long as I'm alive, I'm a liability.

Fred Worthington
Seneca Creek Park, Maryland

Fred's hands shook. Sweat rolled down his face. He felt as if his head would explode. Worthington gulped and tried to get his panic under control. He buried his face in his hands, then took several slow deep breaths, and raised his head.

My future was supposed to be guaranteed.

Fred opened his briefcase and leafed through the file.

If they find me, I'll go to jail.

He lifted the pistol from the briefcase and desperately tried to think of another path of escape.

He shook his head. *There's no way out.*

Fred ran his hand across the soft leather of the car seats.

With renewed resolve, Fred snapped his briefcase shut. He got out of the car, locked the door, and wiped a smudge off the windshield with his sleeve.

Gravel crunched beneath his feet as he walked toward a small grove of trees. Crisp air sharpened his senses. A gentle breeze caressed his face.

Fred sat on a picnic bench, hesitant to move forward. Thoughts whirled through his head.

Fred stood and scanned the area. He walked into the center of a small grove of trees.

It was not my fault.

He raised the gun, cocked it, and gripped the muzzle with his lips.

Isobel
Panama City
October 3, 1989

Rain dripped from the tile roof to the garden path. Isobel enjoyed the steady staccato beat. The sweet scent of flowers drifted into the house on the morning breeze. A small fountain bubbled to provide a lyric accompaniment to the patter of the raindrops.

Isobel looked at her watch and sighed. It was time to go to the office. She paused to enjoy the beauty of her garden. Purple Orquidoas San José. Yellow Papo Amaritto. Flor del Espiritu Santo, the Holy Ghost Orchid. The dove, which gave the orchid its name, was visible. "Bello," she whispered and walked toward her car. Her driver waited, his hand on the door handle.

On the advice of Paola Del Rubin, Isobel hired a driver. Noriega's Dignity Battalions set up roadblocks to harass Americans and wealthy Panamanians. Isobel's driver was a cousin to Juan, Paola's driver.

Traffic was more congested than usual. Police cars with sirens blaring and Noriega's staff cars rushed toward the business district. Isobel huffed. Every day was filled with excessive police activity.

Isobel was surprised to see Roberto at his desk when she got to the office. He didn't come home the night before. Roberto left a message on her office phone saying he would be dining with companions. He'd never arrived at their business this early in the day.

"Why are you here so early?" She leafed through the mail on her desk. "Wasn't your liaison enjoyable last night?"

Roberto didn't answer.

Isobel looked up. *His hands are shaking, and his face is pale.* "What's wrong?"

"We are in trouble."

"What kind of trouble?"

I had an early dinner with a few of our shipping customers last night. They told me some men wanted to speak to me about our Container ships going to New York and Tampa." Roberto pulled a pack of cigarettes from his pocket.

Isobel waited. An uncomfortable heaviness settled in her gut. "Our company ships goods to the United States all the time."

"Not for these people." Roberto's hands shook so badly he couldn't light his cigarette.

"They want us to ship drugs. Tell them to go to hell. You know how I feel about anything that's even remotely related to drugs."

"El Presidente assured them our company would gladly carry their goods."

"So – you think we don't have a choice." Isobel's voice was flat.

"They know we're a well-established shipping company. They know American customs people barely scrutinize our cargo."

"Yes. Because our company is known and trusted. I'd like to keep it that way."

"The men said their boss had a connection in the U. S. State Department. A very highly placed government operative."

"We will NOT smuggle drugs into America."

"Are you listening to me? The Cartel bought a U.S. State Department official." Roberto tried to light his cigarette again. The lighter flew out of his hands.

Sirens wailed on the street below.

Isobel peeked out the window. Jeeps filled with troops raced toward the government office buildings. The sidewalk was empty of pedestrians.

"What else did the gangsters say?"

"If we don't cooperate, they will kill us."

Isobel's secretary entered the room and carefully closed the door. "Madam, excuse me, but my husband just called," she whispered, "American troops are blocking the roads near the Panamanian Defense Force headquarters. Streets are closed."

"Thank you, Miranda. Tell everyone to stay in the building. No one can leave. Tell them not to go near the windows."

The woman nodded and left the room.

"Get yourself together, Roberto. Noriega may fall, but the drug lords will survive, and we'll be at their command – forever."

"What other option do we have?" Roberto gave a resigned shrug and scrambled on the floor to find his lighter.

"Connor Quinlan and his contacts in Washington."

Roberto waved his arms. "Quinlan's a maritime lawyer. How can he help? We have to worry about ourselves. We don't even know how to reach him."

"I can find Connor. I'll try his office, and I'll call Paola. She may have his private phone number."

"What did you do to get on a first-name basis with Quinlan?"

Isobel ignored the insinuation. Her intercom buzzed. "Mr. Riesman is on the telephone, Madam."

"Thank you, put him through." *Why would Eduardo Riesman be calling me?* The phone line clicked, then clicked again. "Eduardo, how good to hear from you. How can this insignificant woman help the editor of La Prensa this morning?"

"This is not the time for flirtation. There has been a coup. Army officers are holding Noriega. If it's true, we'll see a change in government. Right now, Moisés Giraldi is in charge."

Isobel tried to recall the gossip, "He's a major. Part of Noriega's young officers' corps. He's married. I think he has one or two children."

"I'll fill you in when I have more details."

"Thank you, Eduardo." *Could fate be this good to us?* "Roberto, our problem may be resolved. There's been a coup."

Roberto jumped to his feet. "Is Noriega dead?"

"I don't think so. But there has been a coup. Giraldi has assumed control of the government."

The remainder of the day, phone calls and rumors flew. Bankers, merchants, and shippers scurried to gather information.

Roberto's mood wavered between hope and despair.

Early in the evening, Eduardo Riesman called again.

"The coup collapsed. Giraldi had Noriega in custody, but Noriega's National Guard Unit rescued him. Now Giraldi is in Modella."

"What about his family?" Isobel held her breath.

"Giroldi's wife and children are safe. They're in the Canal Zone under the protection of the American Army. Some of Giroldi's officers were able to escape. They're also in the Canal Zone."

"Noriega will torture and kill him."

"He may already be dead," Riesman's voice was gruff. "I'll call again when I know more."

Isobel wiped away tears, walked to Roberto's office, and sat down.

"Is Noriega gone?" Roberto's face held a look of optimism.

"No. The coup failed." She watched all hope leave her husband's face.

Anne
The Institute
October 10, 1989

Anne stared at the pile of patient records on her desk. She glanced at her watch. *Six-thirty.* She dumped the charts in a drawer, secured the lock, and shrugged on her trench coat.

A cold and wet gust of wind blew up the hill from Washington Harbor. Anne shivered, pulled gloves out of her pockets, and increased her stride.

M Street was full of light and people. *Better.* The blinking sign of the neighborhood Italian restaurants caught her eye. *Jimmy's.* Anne stopped short.

The man walking behind her couldn't stop. The collision almost knocked her over. She stifled a scream.

"Sorry, Anne. I didn't expect you to stop short."

Anne whirled, surprised to hear a familiar voice. "Pete? What are you doing here?" She grinned and impetuously hugged him. "Why didn't you call?"

He smiled. "I tried to call you a few weeks ago. Got a message saying your phone was no longer in service."

"I changed my phone number several months ago. What brings you to Georgetown?"

"I'm in town for a class the AMA is giving on political action committees. It's at the Latham."

"Why are you out roaming Georgetown in the cold?"

"I needed some exercise. So, I thought I'd take a walk and find one of the local restaurants. We have a pretty full schedule for the next few days."

"If you like Italian, you've found a good place." Anne pointed to the door to Jimmy's restaurant.

Pete chuckled. "Who doesn't like Italian? I couldn't believe my luck when I saw you. I didn't think I'd catch up to you. You were moving at a pretty good clip."

"I've had a trying day, and the wind coming off the Harbor has me chilled to the bone."

"Have you had dinner yet?"

She shook her head. "I just left work. Thought I'd stop in here."

"Want some company?"

"I would love to have some company. We have a lot to catch up on. How many years has it been?"

"Haven't seen you since the class reunion in 1986."

"Still in Kentucky?'

He nodded. "I'm in Pikeville. I've been as busy with my practice. How about you?"

"Right now, my life is a bit confusing. I'm still doing child psych."

"Every restaurant in Georgetown seems to have a long waiting line."

"This restaurant has some of the finest Italian food in the city. It tastes just like it came from my grandmother's kitchen."

Pete's shoulders slumped. "There's a line here too."

"Not a problem," she whispered and pulled open the restaurant door. "I know the owner."

The proprietor rushed over. "Ah, Dr. Anne. You are here for your seven o'clock reservation a little early. I'm-a have your table ready."

Anne smiled. She didn't have a reservation—the perks of being one of Jimmy's favorite customers.

He ushered them to the only open table for two.

"Thanks, Jimmy, you're a dear." She gave him a peck on the cheek. "One of these days, the customers waiting in line are going to get wise to you."

"You're a good customer, Dr. Anne. For you, I'm-a take the risk."

"Jimmy, this is Pete Miller, one of my classmates from medical school. He's in town for a few days."

"I'm-a please to meet." He nodded to Pete, then skittered off and returned with two glasses of Chateauneuf-du-Pape.

Anne grinned. "Thank you. What are the specials tonight?"

"Two specials tonight." He held up two fingers. "Lobster Diavola and Veal Francais. Either one will have you sighing with pleasure," He turned to Pete, "and will guarantee that you'll return."

Connor
October 10, 1989

Connor stood across the street from the restaurant, hunched against the cold. Hat slouched down, the collar of his trench coat, up. Donovan called him in to discuss his next mission this morning. He'd be leaving for Japan in the morning

He saw the look of delight on Anne's face when she turned to hug Pete.

Bad timing - again.

Connor tugged at the collar of his trench coat.

Looks like she has someone to keep her company.

He turned. Regret sank like a lead weight in his chest. The walk across the M Street Bridge seemed miles long.

Maybe it's better this way.

The Foggy Bottom Metro Station's escalator carried him down to the subway platform.

Anne
October 24, 1989

Anne walked up the steps to the Institute. It was her first day back to work after a medical conference in New Orleans.

I feel like I've been on a treadmill for the past month.

"Good Morning, Dr. Anne."

"Good Morning, Maggie. How are you today?"

Maggie frowned. "Do you have a minute?"

"Of course. What's the matter?"

"I don't want to talk about this out here."

Anne frowned. Was Maggie about to quit? "I have lots of time." She unlocked her office door.

Maggie followed Anne and closed the door behind her. She sat on the edge of the chair across from Anne and took a deep breath. "A man's called you every day this week. He sounds – mean – and ugly."

Prickles of fear crept up Anne's spine. She smiled to help ease Maggie's fears. "Probably just a disgruntled parent. What's his name and number?"

"He refuses to leave his name or a number you can call to reach him."

"Did he indicate the reason for his call?"

"No. He said, you've never met him – but you've met some of his friends."

Anne shivered. "Did this person say why he wanted to talk to me?"

"He wants you to convey a message.

"Did he threaten you?"

"Not exactly, but he threatened you." Maggie handed Anne several memos. "I took some notes."

Anne read the hastily written messages. "He wants me to send a message to someone, and he wants me to tell him where 'my friend' is." She shuddered when she read the next note. "If I know what's good for me, I'll cooperate." Anne looked at Maggie. "Mean and ugly? Sinister is the word I'd use."

"Sinister. Yes, sinister is the word I was looking for."

Anne's phone rang.

"Good Morning, thank you for calling the –"

"Good Morning, Dr. Damiano," the man growled. "I'm glad to see you're finally back in the office."

"Do you wish to speak to Dr. Damiano?"

"Don't try to bullshit me. I know who I'm talking to." The Hispanic accented growl continued.

Anne's stomach fluttered. She exhaled slowly. "Yes, this is Dr. Damiano. How can I help you?"

"Your friend knows who I represent. I got a message for him. Tell him he better lay off, or he's going to be sorry he messed with *my* men. I'm sure he doesn't want you to get hurt. He'd better follow our instructions. If he ignores this message, he'll be very sorry, and so will you."

"I have no plans to see Mr. Quinlan. I haven't seen him in over a month. And I have no idea where he is." Anne forced her voice to be quiet and even.

"Don't give me that crap. Give Quinlan this message. Either he comes out of hiding, or you'll get another visit from us. This time you'll both lose. He'll have a whole lot more than a dislocated shoulder. And, you'll have more than just slashed tires."

Anne heard a click and then the dial tone.

She stared at the receiver for a long moment.

"Dr. Anne? Are you okay?"

"What? Oh, Maggie."

"You look pale."

"The phone call was upsetting." Anne glanced at her watch. "I need to make a call. Would you mind bringing me a cup of coffee, please?"

"No problem." Maggie rushed from the room.

Anne dialed Connor's office.

Angela
October 25, 1989

Angela stared at the calendar. She started to count the days since she'd heard from her boss. The phone jolted from her musings. "Hi, Angela. This is Anne Damiano. May I speak to Mr. Quinlan?"

"He's not here, Dr. Damiano. I don't know when he'll be back. I haven't heard from him for several days."

"Can you get a message to him? It's important."

"I'll call his pager and leave a message for him to call me. But then I have to wait for him to call in."

"Please, when you hear from him, ask him to call me. Tell him it's essential."

Angela frowned as she placed the receiver in the phone cradle. *Dr. Anne's usually so happy and lighthearted.*

She paged Connor and added the 'crucial' code to the call back number.

Within minutes the phone rang.

"I didn't expect you to get back to me this fast. Angela…''

"Hello –? May I speak to Angela Pisacano? This is the Emergency Room at Presbyterian Hospital."

"This is Ms. Pisacano. How can I help you?" Angela held her breath.

"Your mother was brought to the Emergency Department with chest pain about a half-hour ago. She's asking for you. Can you come to the hospital?"

"Yes, yes. I'll be right there."

Angela quickly turned off her computer and locked her desk. She grabbed her purse and coat.

"Ruth, Mom's been taken to the hospital. They need me there right away."

Angela ran down the hall to the bank of elevators before Ruth could respond.

Connor

Traffic was at a dead stop when Connor's pager buzzed. He read the code. Angela. Important. *I wonder what's happened.*

Connor was in the northbound lane of the New Jersey Turnpike. He had just crossed the Delaware River. The line of cars in front of him stretched as far as he could see. There was no way to legally or illegally to cross to the southbound lane. *I won't be getting to a phone any time soon. I hope it's something that can wait.*

Half an hour later, Connor's lane of traffic had inched far enough for him to take the first exit. He turned left on Hawks Bridge Road and called the office from a convenient store payphone.

Ruth answered the call.

"Hi Ruth, this is Mr. Quinlan. Angela paged me a while ago. I was on the Turnpike. Is she there?"

"No, sir, Angela's gone for the day. She got a phone call from the hospital. The ambulance took her mother to the Emergency Room. Angela ran when she got the call."

"What happened?"

"Angela didn't say. She looked pretty upset."

"Do you know which hospital?"

"No, she just said her mother was taken to the hospital and ran out."

"Thanks, Ruth. I'm sure she'll catch up with me later." *She never uses the code for an immediate callback unless it's essential.* "She didn't leave any kind of message?"

"Wait, maybe there's a note on her desk." Connor could hear Ruth shuffling papers. "Just the beginning of a note. All it says is Doctor. She didn't write down the name. It was probably the call from the hospital."

Angela

The Coronary Intensive Care Unit doctors said Angela's mother had a myocardial event.

What the heck is an event? Angela remained at the bedside for several hours. Finally, her brother, Joe, arrived.

"Sorry it took me so long to get here. There was an accident on the Long Island Expressway. How's Mom?"

Angela filled him in. "They're sure Mom's had significant heart damage." Tears rolled down Angela's face.

Joe pulled out his handkerchief and blotted her cheeks. Have you had anything to eat?"

"Not since breakfast."

"Go on down to the coffee shop and get a bite."

Angela rode the elevator to the Lobby. *I didn't give Mr. Quinlan the message from Dr. Anne.*

She stepped off the elevator and moved toward the bank of phone booths.

"Code Blue, CCU – Code Blue, CCU." The announcement blared two more times over the hospital intercom.

Angela took the stairs two at a time.

Her brother caught her hand as she charged down the hall toward the unit. "No one can go in."

"Is it Mom?"

"I don't know. All of a sudden, buzzers went off. The nurses herded everyone out when the arrest team charged through the doors."

Ninety minutes later, the Cardiac Arrest Team exited Coronary Care. When they wheeled the crash cart out of the Unit, the medical and nursing staff circled one of the families in the waiting room.

"Go home and get some rest." Joe was adamant.

"But…"

"They gave Mom a sleeping pill. I can stay the night. I'll call if anything happens."

Angela reluctantly agreed. She shrugged into her coat and kissed her mother. "You be good," she whispered. "I'll be back in the morning."

Angela glanced at the clock. *Quarter after ten. I wonder if Mr. Quinlan ever got the message.*

Angela

At ten minutes before midnight, Angela sighed with relief and sank into the sofa in her living room. *What a day.* She checked her watch. *It's way too late to call Ruth.*

Angela dialed Connor's beeper leaving her home number and the code that signaled call back. She walked to the kitchen to fix a cup of tea. The kitchen phone rang as she turned on the gas under the tea kettle.

"Boss?"

"How's your mom? How are you?"

"Mom is in the Coronary Care Unit. She's dodged another bullet. Did Ruth give you the message from Dr. Damiano?"

"Ruth didn't say anything about a message from Dr. Damiano."

"Dr. Anne wanted to talk to you. Said it was important. She sounded upset."

Connor
Washington, DC
October 26, 1989

Connor reached the large wooden double doors of Van Houten and Dewitt. The oak doors and gold lettering proclaimed the firm was old, established, and stable.

His unique knowledge and connections with the international shipping community was a valuable commodity. Although Connor spent most of his time at his office in the World Trade Center in New York, he was an associate of the esteemed Washington firm. Two senior members of the firm were former high-level government officials. One had been a former Transportation Department Secretary and the other an official at the Central Intelligence Agency.

After Connor spoke to Angela, he drove back to Washington. He checked into the J.W. Marriott at 3:00 a.m. and decided it was far too late to call Anne.

Connor unlocked his office, slid into the Moroccan leather chair, and pulled the phone toward him, and dialed Anne's number.

Anne picked up on the second ring.

"Sorry I didn't call sooner. Angela had to leave work early yesterday. I didn't get your message until very late last night."

She gave him the details of the phone call. "I was chilled to the bone by his voice. Who are these people who hate you so much?"

Connor's fists clenched. "What did he say exactly?"

"He said we would both be in danger if you didn't quit messing with his people."

Someone threatened Anne, again. He didn't speak for a long minute.

"Connor? Are you still there?"

"Oh, sorry. Do you still treat the daughter of Señor Empañada?"

"Yes. How do you know that Empañada's daughter is one of my patients?"

"Don't ask. I know you're one of Helena's doctors. I need to speak to Señor Empañada. Do you think you can arrange a meeting?"

"It's Saturday. I have his private phone number. I'll try to reach him." She paused. "What does Señor Empañada have to do with this?"

Connor didn't respond.

Anne sighed. "Where can I reach you?"

"I'm at Van Houten and DeWitt. I'll be here all day."

Connor's next call was to Donovan.

"Donovan, I've had it. These bastards never learn. Anne Damiano got a threatening phone call yesterday. We need to roll up this operation soon. The SOBs are operating in Washington under everyone's noses. Losing two punks didn't teach them."

"Connor, calm down. Things *are* moving. Slowly, but moving."

"Only if you consider crawling forward movement. The Cartel has to know the information I brought back is already in play."

"Give it time."

"Time? How much time?"

"Not much Fred Worthington's body was found in Seneca Park this morning."

"Guess the Cartel realized he was a liability."

"Looks like suicide."

"Suicide? Are you sure?"

"Forensics said everything points to a self-inflicted wound. His fingerprints were on the gun. The body wasn't moved. His car was fifty feet away, in the parking lot."

"Damn. Did Worthington leave a note?"

"No, but he left a ton of information. His briefcase was in the car. He kept good records, as all turncoats seem to do. We're positive the Columbians didn't kill him."

"Who else was working with him?"

"I haven't gotten a full report. Hopefully, the files will point us to any accomplices."

"How much time do you need?"

"I'm pretty sure we'll be able to activate our plan in December."

"I'll keep in touch. In the meantime, who do I talk to about getting some protection for Anne? You or the FBI?"

"I'll take care of it."

"Okay. I'll let Anne know so she doesn't panic when she sees even more men following her."

"Do you think I should arrange for a female agent to stay with her?"

"You could try, but I doubt she would accept the offer."

The intercom buzzed as soon as Connor hung up. "A Doctor Damiano's on the phone, Mr. Quinlan."

"Put the call through, please." Connor listened to the clicks. "Hi, Anne, how'd you do with Empañada?"

"He agreed to meet with you in my office this afternoon."

"Your office? Is that a good idea?"

"His demand. Three o'clock."

"Thanks, Wiggles."

"Meet me in the Institute parking garage. I'll let you in the office."

"See you then."

Connor sat back and looked out the window on K Street. *We have to get rid of these damn thugs.* He bowed his head and rubbed his forehead. *I trust Donovan, but I just don't trust the system.*

He made one more phone call.

"Paul Garcia......"

"Paul, I need a favor."

Mateo Empañda

Mateo Empañada waited in Anne's office. A few minutes before three, Anne and Connor entered the room.

"Señor, I'd like you to meet…"

Empañada stood. "Mr. Quinlan's reputation precedes him," He extended his hand. "I'm glad we could meet."

"Anne, would you excuse us?" Connor's voice was firm.

She left the office and closed the door quietly behind her.

Empañada knew Connor was associated with the CIA. *Quinlan is a man not easily intimidated.*

"My curiosity brought me here today. What business could you possibly have with me, Mr. Quinlan?"

"Please, call me Connor. May I call you Mateo?"

Empañada smiled and nodded. He was relieved. The meeting wa*sn't going to be adversarial.*

Connor sat on the edge of Anne's desk and gestured to the chair. "My sources tell me Doctor Damiano is one of your daughter's physicians. Our meeting has nothing to do with your daughter. I asked you to come here because I want to prevent any further threats to Dr. Damiano."

Empañada considered the situation. He knew the drug lords were unhappy with Quinlan. He also knew about the attempt to kidnap Anne and Trish.

Empañada walked a fine line with illegality, but he was no fan of Noriega. In Columbia's closed society, he had no choice but to maintain a working relationship with the Cartel.

"Doctor Damiano is helping my daughter. I have no intention of harming her."

"I think you know what I'm talking about. I'm sure you have no personal interest in harming the doctor. We each have powerful resources. I hope they can work together to keep Dr. Damiano safe."

Empañada kept his expression neutral.

"Please carry a message to – certain people. If anyone hurts Anne Damiano in any way, I will make sure they, and their entire operation, are brought down. They will be hunted down and killed, and we will not spare their families. Dr. Damiano is a non-player.

They must understand what will happen if they make war on an innocent bystander."

Empañada's eyebrows moved up a micro–millimeter. He nodded in agreement and smiled. "I think we could be friends, Connor. As long as you don't mind having a compadre who may have an occasional dubious dealing."

Connor laughed. "You should meet some of my clients, and more than a few of my associates on the waterfront."

"The cartel bosses are purecos – pigs. Their single focus is wealth. They're willing to poison the world to enlarge their purses. They hurt business for everyone. Some of my dealings may be a little, how do you say, shady. But I am not like them."

Connor crossed his arms.

"In South America, we learn to live and let live. As long as they don't bother me, I don't bother them." He gave a quick nod. "I will carry your message. They'll want something to save face."

Connor nodded. Tell them Manuel Noriega will be history."

Empañada stood and extended his hand. "Be careful, Connor. These men are ruthless."

Connor shrugged. "They'll have to plan alternatives for their operations in Panama. Perhaps a warning will be appreciated. Trying to get me is fair game. Using Dr. Damiano as bait for their scheme cannot be allowed."

"Doctor Damiano is a fine woman."

"I hope you will help me protect her."

"I will do all in my power."

They shook hands again.

"Tell me, Connor, how did you know I would not notify the cartel about our meeting?"

"I did my homework. You don't admire the cartel. Nevertheless, I took precautions. if you look carefully, you will notice more than a few government agents in the vicinity."

Empañada shook his head. "Despite your research, you had no faith in me."

"They pose no danger to you. And, I assume you brought your contingency with you."

Empañada gave a quick shoulder shrug and head nod.

"My people are guarding Anne." Connor gave a small smile. "As soon as you leave, I'll call to let them know we've reached an amicable agreement."

Empañada laughed and patted Connor on the shoulder.

He left the office and entered to lobby.

Anne sat in a chair near the elevators.

Empañada kissed Anne's hand and headed for the exit.

Anne

Anne walked back to her office. "What on earth did you say to him?" Her brow furrowed. "He's a different person. Suddenly he's a gentleman."

"We found something we agree on."

Anne crossed her arms. "And what might that be?"

"Just a work of art we both admire."

"Mateo Empañada has agreed to be my new best friend. By the way, he likes you, too."

"And you agree on a work of art?" Anne asked.

"Oh, yes, indeed. A beautiful one." He smiled. "Things are getting pretty hot again. You'll have protection until everything gets taken care of."

Anne squared her shoulders. "Protection? What makes you think I need protection?"

"Don't get your back up. I'd prefer not to have a replay of last month." Connor opened the door. "Stay happy, Wiggles. I'm sorry you got mixed up in all this. Hope he gives you everything you deserve."

Connor was out the door before Anne could answer.

"What on earth are you talking about?" she said as the door latch click into place. "Who do you think is going to give me everything I deserve?"

Connor
November 10, 1989

Connor entered his office in New York. He knuckle rapped Angela's desk as he passed it. "Mornin,' Angela."

Angela's early morning memos and notes waited on his desk. Three urgent messages from Isobel Duarte were at the top of the list. 'I must see you. You can reach me at the St. Regis.'

"Coffee, Boss?"

"Nope – but thanks." He pulled his trench coat back on. "I've got an appointment."

"Where are you going?"

"To the Saint Regis Hotel." He left his office and took the elevator to the Forty-fourth floor, then changed to an express elevator that carried him to the lobby of the World Trade Center. The system of elevators was intriguing and ingenious. The architects designed the towers to maximize space for revenue-producing tenants.

Connor dashed down the steps.

The fastest and most efficient way of traveling through New Your City is by subway. Crosstown traffic coagulated into a seemingly immovable tangle of vehicles that could test the patience of any traveler. It inspired creative profanities from the multilingual drivers. The E train access from the concourse of the Trade Center carried Connor close to Fifth Avenue and the Saint Regis Hotel.

If ever there was a statement about capitalism and the benefits of a free society, it was Fifth Avenue.

An ardent communist from China or Russia would have difficulty believing this much wealth and opulence was available to the masses. In many countries, the cost of a single purchase from any shop on Fifth Avenue could support a family for a year.

Crowds of New Yorkers moved along the sidewalks at a fast pace. They were oblivious to the elegant facades and the decorations. Only tourists slowed to stare in the windows.

Connor turned east on Fifty-fifth Street and stood for a few seconds to admire the stately Saint Regis Hotel. A remnant of a bygone era but still as fashionable as when it opened. He walked into the gilded beaux art lobby and looked for a house phone. Off to one side, he saw the Astor Lounge. Connor started to sing softly. "Have you heard 'bout Mimmsie Star – she got pinched in the Ass – Tor bar. Well, Did You Evah – what a swell party this is."

Several people turned to watch him.

Maybe I should leave the singing to Frank Sinatra.

Isobel picked up the phone on the third ring.

"Hello, Isobel, this is Connor. Meet me in the lounge."

"Come to my suite. 1501. It would be better if our conversation isn't public."

Isobel, dressed in a tight dark blue skirt and a sheer white blouse, opened the door as soon as Connor knocked.

She hugged him as he entered the room. "Thank you for coming. Please sit down."

Isobel took Connor's trench coat and put it over the back of a chair, then sat across from him.

"Can I call room service for some coffee or drinks?"

"Nothing for me, thanks. What's happened?"

"I came from Panama just to speak to you in person. Paola agreed you might be able to help me. She trusts you. Can you help me?"

"Isobel, I can't help you until you tell me what's wrong."

"Our shipping business deals with all sorts of people; some are evil. The Cartel has threatened Roberto. They know we have connections in Columbia and Panama, as well as the United States. They want us to conceal drug shipments."

"How?"

"They want us to put the drugs in the containers with legitimate shipments from South and Central America. It is a ploy they use to take over companies. They will squeeze us out. There is no one for us to turn to in Panama. If we go to the wrong people, we are dead."

"Who is threatening you? What method will they use?"

Isobel wrung her hands and walked to the window.

"The Cartel knows the American authorities don't search every container coming into your ports. The customs people have a system for selecting the containers they decide to search. Because we are well-known and trusted shippers, the Columbians know the authorities rarely search our containers."

Connor nodded, "Customs uses profiling to target shipments based on origins, destinations, and the identity of the shippers. Big companies who routinely ship large amounts to known receivers seldom have their containers opened and searched. There are too many containers coming into our ports for customs to do a thorough job. Customs singles out shipments from unknowns."

Isobel paced, ran her fingers through her hair, swiped at tears. That is precisely why they contacted us. We transship cargo from all over Latin America and consolidate the freight in Panama."

"So, the containers won't be sealed until after they put the drugs in."

"Yes. The drugs come to Panama from Columbia. Noriega's people are happy to accept the pittance the Cartel pays them."

"Do they want you to get involved in moving the money?"

Isobel twisted her rings and shook her head. "They launder the money by faking transactions. They hide the drugs in the shipments, sell the cheap goods in the United States, then deposit the money in a Panamanian bank. We wouldn't be part of the money-laundering scheme – they only expect us to ship the drugs. One search will ruin us."

"Are they only using consolidated shipments? Do they have an interest in other kinds of shipments as well?"

Isobel pointed out the window.

"Right now, in Brooklyn, they're unloading coffee and cocoa. It would be easy to hide drugs in those shipments. We ship coffee from Columbia."

Connor knew the docks had been used for years to import all sorts of illegal goods. The New York Waterfront Commission was effective in controlling crime committed on the docks. High jacking, kickbacks, pilferage, and loan sharking were almost a thing of the past.

"Isobel, my contacts will want your cooperation. If we're lucky, there will be changes in Panama. If you cooperate with the Columbians, they *will* take over your business. You'll be caught smuggling narcotics and take the fall. If you don't cooperate, they'll kill you and Roberto."

Isobel nodded resignedly.

"Would you able to track a specific container used to move the drugs?"

Isobel stopped pacing and sat in a chair facing him. She wrinkled her brow. "Yes, our computer system tracks each shipment and can tell us the location of each container. We would know which containers they use. And we would know its destination."

"Would you be willing to assist the authorities by giving them information?"

Isobel wiped a tear away.

She tossed her head. "Yes, I will."

"It could be dangerous."

She looked up with a smile that never reached her eyes. "The only alternatives I see are to either lose our business or die."

Connor stood, "I'll have someone get in touch with you. He'll be from the Justice Department. He can be trusted. He'll set up a system you can use to provide the information. Don't tell Roberto what you're doing. He might talk too much."

"You're right. But it will be difficult to keep this information from him."

"Tell Roberto the problem's resolved. Tell him he'll be safe if he doesn't know the details."

"I will never let these men get control." She reached for Connor's hands. "I knew you would have an answer for us. I am so afraid. Just feel my heart beating."

Connor flushed and pulled his hands away. "Isobel, concentrate on business. I'm going back to my office to start the arrangements." Connor slipped on his trench coat and kissed Isobel's cheek.

"Someone will call you. It will be a man named Garcia or someone who works with him."

Anne
November 21, 1989

Anne looked at the clock. It was time to leave.

She breathed a sigh of relief, ready for a long weekend at the cottage.

Her intercom buzzed. "Dr. Damiano, there's a man here to see you."

"I wasn't expecting anyone. I was just about to leave. Who is it?"

"He says his name is Donovan. He's a friend of Connor Quinlan."

"Tell him to come in, please." Anne felt a prickle of fear. *Has something happened to Connor?*

A tall, well-built man with a receding hairline entered her office, the kind of man who dominates any room.

She reached out to shake his hand. "How do you do, Mr. Donovan. How can I help you? Have I done something to upset your watchdogs?"

A surprisingly soft voice answered. "No, of course not. I have something I'd like to discuss with you."

Anne's eyebrows shot up. She gestured to a chair. "Discuss? With me? Has something happened to Connor?"

Donovan smiled and nodded but remained standing. "No – Connor is fine. I read the after-action report of the Newcomb incident. You stayed very cool and calm."

"Cool and calm on the outside, perhaps. My insides were jangling like mad."

"You were able to assist Quinlan and Oratchewski with your actions and quick thinking."

"Well, I didn't know about Mr. Oratchewski, and it didn't take a genius to realize someone was outside at the power box. I hoped it was Connor."

"You stayed collected. And, your reasoning was better than most people would have shown - considering the circumstances. Connor thinks highly of you, as do your friends, Stuart and William."

"Oh, right. Stuart and William worked with you too."

"They were associated with several intelligence agencies many years ago. Which brings me to the reason I'm here today."

Anne's eyebrow rose again.

"I've looked over your Curriculum Vitae. I was pleased to see you had interests beyond psychiatry. But your psychiatric training added a big plus to my decision. You're an MD, of course, and you've also pursued a degree in Public Health. Impressive."

Anxious to get home before dark, Anne checked her watch. "Where is this conversation going, Mr. Donovan?"

"I've also spoken to Director Frye. He's filled me in on several situations you've handled well. I'd like you to consider a position with my organization. I think you and Quinlan would make one hell of a team."

Anne stared in disbelief.

"What would I do with my practice? I'm not like Connor. I can't just leave for a week or more at a moment's notice."

"Think about it. If you decide to join us, we'll work out details."

"What about training?"

"If you decided to join us, you'll be trained. *Very* well trained."

A full minute passed.

Donovan finally broke the silence. "Please, think about it. Consider working with us."

Anne stood and extended her hand. "I can't promise you anything. But I will think about it, Mr. Donovan."

"I'll contact you in a few weeks." He shook her hand and left.

Anne shrugged on her trench coat. Then stopped and dialed the director's office.

"Hello, Sir. I would like to take more than a long weekend. My life is in a bit of turmoil right now. I would like to use up some of my vacation days to think things through."

"I was afraid you would ask me for more time off. Of course, you can take the week off. You have more vacation days coming than anyone in the institute."

"Thank you, sir."

She hung up the phone, picked up her briefcase, and headed for the door.

"See you next month, Cindy."

"Next month? Won't you be here next week?"

"No – I'm taking some time off. Have a great Thanksgiving."

"You too, Dr. Anne."

Anne
Georgetown

Anne glanced out her window.

Her anger overflowed. *There's another one. Every time I turn around, there's one more strange man outside.*

Anne flew around the townhouse, putting things away, dusting, and vacuuming. She scrubbed the kitchen floor with a vengeance, then walked into her study. *What a mess. I haven't cleaned off this desk or straightened up since Lenny and Trish were here.*

Anne methodically scanned the piles of papers and mail on her desk.

I feel like a caged mouse.

Most of the mail was junk. A few bills. Then a clean white envelope.

Anne

Connor's writing. She tore open the seal and began to read:

'I remember the Christmas dances at St. Benedicts. Father Eugene played the piano. We'd stand around the big tree and sing Christmas carols. So many beautiful memories.

I also remember Christmases at strange outposts when I was in the military. Dirt and dust. A hot and humid Christmas when I felt abandoned and wondered if I'd ever see you again.'

The note made Anne's throat ache. She wandered to the kitchen, unable to get her bearings, then returned to her office to read the letter again.

When did Connor leave this here?

She narrowed her eyes and ran up the stairs, then peeked out her bedroom window, again.

Anne grabbed a suitcase from the closet.

Anne
November 22, 1989

Anne woke refreshed and relaxed. Reluctant to get out from under her down coverlet, she pulled the blanket to her chin and snuggled.

She lingered over her coffee and planned her next moves.

At ten o'clock, she washed the breakfast dishes, dressed, and started her drive to the Eastern Shore.

With a glance in her rearview mirror, she noted two cars. They left their regular parking places: a black sedan, and a standard US government issue, dark gray Ford Taurus.

Anne drove directly to St. Michaels. She strolled along Talbot Street and paused to use shop windows to determine who was following her. *Four guys.* Two of the men wore windbreakers over white shirts, casual slacks, and loafers. They didn't look any different than the locals and visitors to St. Michaels. The other two wore black suits and wing-tipped shoes.

She spent the morning in St. Michaels. A stop at the Christmas Shop where bought several ornaments, then drove to the Maritime Museum to purchase a Hooper Straight Lighthouse ornament.

Better get some lunch.

The Town Dock was pleasantly warm.

"Table for one, Dr. Anne?"

"Yes, it's just me today."

Anne waited until all her shadows settled at tables in the restaurant. She placed her order, left her coat and packages at the table, then walked to the ladies' room. On her way back, she made a call from the public phone.

"Bentley Inn."

"Hello, this is Anne – um - Anne Romano. I'm hoping to visit Bay Head in a few days. Do you have any rooms available next week?"

"Are you traveling alone?"

"Yes."

"A single room will be vacant on Monday. It has a bath."

"Great. Please reserve the room for Anne – Anne Romano. R-O-M-A-N-O. See you next week."

Anne hung up before they could ask for a credit card to confirm the reservation.

Almost blew it! I can't register under my real name – Mom's maiden should suffice for now. With any luck, they'll think I'm an airhead and hold the room.

She returned to her table, pulled a novel out of her purse, and sat back.

On the walk back to her car, Anne passed Stuart and William's house. She ducked into the shadows of a large holly tree, then slid quietly along the side of the house. When she got to their back garden, she hid between the holly tree and the back wall.

Let's see if I can give my shadows the slip.

Anne heard hurried footsteps and curses from the men trying to find her.

When everything was quiet, she knocked on Stuart's kitchen window. He opened the back door.

"What's with the cloak and dagger behavior?"

Anne acted surprised. "I came through your back garden from the Town Dock. When I saw you leaning over the sink, I knocked on the window to get your attention."

"Scared the daylights out of me." Stuart heaved a deep breath.

"I've been wandering around town all morning. Thought I'd stop in and find out what I can add to tomorrow's dinner."

"We're fixing a traditional Thanksgiving dinner. Whatever you'd like to add would be fine."

"My mother made a terrific whole-berry cranberry sauce." She tapped the kitchen counter. "And, the family recipe for pumpkin pie is outstanding."

"Sounds great. We'll start dinner at around two in the afternoon. Several neighbors are joining us for dessert and coffee. Plan on staying for the evening."

"I'd better make *two* pumpkin pies."

Anne went out the back door, crossed the park, and walked along Willow Street until she was sure her shadows were all in place.

She drove to Easton, stopped at the bank, then went to the supermarket.

Back at the cottage, she boiled cranberries and baked pumpkin pies.

After dinner, she cleaned out the fireplace, then placed logs and tinder. She swept and dusted the cottage and cleaned the kitchen.

Late in the evening, she put on a warm jacket and sat out on the screened porch with a blanket over her legs. The moon was a sliver in the sky. Even the heavens were helping.

Anne
Thanksgiving Day

At one-thirty, Anne packed her contributions to the Thanksgiving dinner into the car and drove to St. Michaels.

During dinner, Anne quizzed Stuart and William about their past. Their answers were vague. Frustrated, she put down her fork, folded her napkin, and cleared her throat. "Okay, you two. You've been avoiding my questions long enough. I want to know why none of you, Connor included, told me you knew one another when I first introduced you. You've known one another for a long time."

The men looked at one another, then shrugged.

"That night at the cottage when the men tried to get Connor, he told me to call you. You both knew Ora. And, you knew what to do, who to call, and how to keep the whole situation quiet."

"We did what needed to be done," Stuart offered.

"Why didn't you tell me you knew Connor when I first introduced him to you?"

Stuart blinked. "You had no need to know."

"What's *that* supposed to mean?"

Stuart smiled at his partner. "William, would you pass the cranberry sauce, please." He turned to Anne. "You must give me this recipe. I hope it's not a family secret."

"Don't change the subject. You knew Mr. Oratchewski as well."

"What do you put in the cranberry sauce? There's a hint of some other flavor."

Anne rolled her eyes. "Oh, for goodness sake. Orange zest *and* lemon zest." She looked from William to Stuart.

William looked down at his plate.

Stuart closed his eyes and acted as if cranberry sauce was ambrosia.

The pieces of their story started to fall into place. Anne pointed her fork at Stuart. "You know Connor and Ora because you *all* worked for the CIA."

Stuart shook his head, "We never worked for the CIA – specifically."

Anne's mind went into a whirl. *Not part of the CIA? South America is the one place they have in common.* "You told me you ran an Import-Export business in Bogotá."

"We had a shop in Bogotá. We exported porcelain ware. How long do you boil the cranberries?"

"Till they burst." Frustrated with their evasions, she gritted her teeth. "Oratchewski doesn't seem to be the type of person Connor would normally have as a friend or business associate. And, Connor certainly doesn't hang around porcelain shops."

Finally, Stuart spoke. "How many of Connor's friends have you met, Anne?"

"I knew all the guys from St. Benedict's Prep and some from St. Peter's College. And, of course, all the gang from down the shore."

Stuart shook his head. "No, I'm talking about his current associates and acquaintances."

"I know his secretary, and I've met one or two of the lawyers at the World Trade Center."

"Anyone else?"

"No." Anne blinked. "Connor hasn't introduced me to anyone in years." Anne fiddled with her napkin. "I guess you two must be some of his **other** friends." The tone of her voice conveyed certainty.

William and Stuart glanced at each other. Stuart nodded.

"William agreed. "We've known Connor for many years."

Anne closed her eyes to concentrate on Stuart's response. She blinked as the answer came to her. *Connor was in Army Intelligence before he became a CIA operative.* "Connor and Oratchewski were a team in the military. And, you two," she waved her knife at Stuart and William, "you were in Army Intelligence. Your shop was the cover for a safe house."

Their silence affirmed her suspicion.

"Can you at least tell me if you liked working undercover?"
More silence.

"I have a good reason for asking. It's not just idle curiosity. I had an offer from someone named Donovan. I'm trying to figure out what to do with the rest of my life."

Stuart took a deep breath, "Alright. I don't know if 'like' is the word I would use. I believe in our government. Our country. If I could serve in some capacity now, I would. We made a difference. *We* had a relatively passive role. *Connor,* on the other hand…"

"You've said enough," William injected.

"More things I don't need to know. I wish you still ran a safe house. I could use one."

"Are you in danger?"

Anne shrugged. "I don't know," she sighed. "I feel like a specimen. The bad guys are watching me. The good guys are watching the bad guys watch me. It's driving me crazy."

The doorbell startled them.

Stuart looked at his watch. "Must be the neighbors."

William strode to the door to greet the friends.

"Hope you haven't eaten all the pumpkin pie," one of the newcomers exclaimed.

"What's the coffee of the day?" another asked.

"Let's all go to the living room," William began to clear the table.

"Here, let me help."

"I'll put out the dessert dishes and silverware."

"Where's the whipped cream?"

Total confusion reigned until the dessertsdeserts were selected, and the coffee and liqueurs poured.

Everyone gathered around the fireplace in the living room.

The chatter and the company distracted Anne. As she was leaving, William whispered in her ear.

She nodded.

Anne
November 24, 1989

Friday morning, Anne drove to the hardware store in Easton to purchase supplies.

Back at the cottage, she removed the screen door hinges, patched the holes in the screen, put new hardware on the frame, and re-hung the door. Then she tackled the laundry room doors. By midday, there was no evidence of Herb's presence.

William stopped by on his way to Easton. "The house's looking good."

"Thanks – I've been patching and painting all day. Tea?"

"If you have time."

Anne brewed the tea and set out cookies. "You said you have an idea."

William nodded. "Do you really need a safe house?"

A thrill of excitement shot through Anne. "I need time to think. Away from constant observance. Do you know a place I can stay?"

William explained his scheme.

She nodded. "Sounds perfect."

After William left, Anne canceled her reservations at the Bentley Inn. She began to dial another number, stopped, and gently set the receiver in its cradle. *No advanced reservations. I'll have to leave my success to luck.*

Anne packed a suitcase, stored it in the trunk of the car, and turned off the overhead light.

Anne
Monday Morning
November 27, 1989

Anne woke at 3:00 a.m. and dressed in the dark. Black turtleneck sweater, black slacks. With a smile of satisfaction, she pulled the black hooded sweatshirt she purchased at the hardware store over her head.

She locked the cottage door. There was no evidence of any of the men watching her between the house and the highway.

Thankful for her midnight blue car, she drove without turning on her headlights to Highway 33 and turned left. She didn't turn her car lights on until she crossed the Oak Creek Bridge. Then she accelerated and drove toward Easton.

A glance in her rearview mirror as she merged onto Highway 50 confirmed two cars were speeding toward her.

She slowed down, crossed the Chesapeake Bay Bridge, and meandered on state and county roads until she reached State Highway 108, a little south of Ellicott City.

Her drive continued through Columbia, then Crossville, and continued west.

The two cars kept pace.

At the Montgomery County line, she stomped on the gas pedal, went around a right curve, doused her headlights, and took the sharp left onto Tucker Lane.

The gradient was steep. Anne took her foot off the gas pedal, then almost lost control with a quick right turn onto a dirt road. She allowed the car to drift to a stop. When she was positive the other vehicles didn't turn onto Tucker Lane, she drove slowly along the narrow dirt road. A small service road branched to the right. Anne turned, parked in a grove of trees, and waited.

She pulled on black gloves, got out of the car, and crept through the woods. There were no vehicles on Tucker Lane. Her pursuers didn't make the turn.

Ron Johnson, CIA

"Where'd she go?" Ron Johnson took his foot off the gas.

"She's probably way ahead. She must've gunned it."

Ron rounded another curve. He pointed straight ahead. "Taillights. Gotta be her." He sped toward the vehicle

"Damn. It's an old pick-up truck. We better go back and make sure there wasn't a side road."

"I think we passed a driveway."

"I didn't see any driveway."

"On the left side of the road. There was a crooked wooden fence and what looked like a driveway just about the time Anne took off."

Ron turned and drove back along Highway 108.

"It's not a driveway. It's a road. Dr. Damiano must've turned here. The grade on this road is so steep we didn't see her. She's probably long gone."

"There's a chance we could catch up with her." He pressed hard on the gas.

"Take it easy, Ron."

Ron ignored his partner and continued to drive with abandon, narrowly missing stone walls, and massive trees. He screeched to a halt at a stop sign. "Connecticut Avenue." He pounded the dashboard. "Damn it."

"We better call Donovan."

Donovan

"What do you mean you lost her?" Donovan growled.

"She drove down a county highway. She was taking her time. Then all of a sudden, she accelerated, went around a curve, and disappeared."

"You let her get out of your sight."

"No – she disappeared. She lost us. If she took the road, we think she took. She's lucky to be alive. It was a sharp turn. She was driving like a bat out of hell."

"Did you go back to follow the road to find out where it goes?"

"We did. The road's a little more than a mile long. It ends at Connecticut Ave. She was long gone. Even if we knew which way to turn, we wouldn't catch-up."

"Damn. If you can't find her, I hope the thugs can't find her either."

"They're as confused as we are. The other guys were right behind us."

Connor

Connor was startled out of a dream when the phone rang. "Hullo?"

"We lost her."

Connor was instantly awake. "Donovan?" Fear gripped Connor's chest. He glanced at the clock. It was almost 6:00 a.m. "Lost her? Empañada assured me those guys wouldn't kidnap her."

"They didn't. Anne initiated her own escape."

"What?"

"Anne left the cottage at three a.m., took all the men following her on a jaunt from Newcomb through Columbia, and managed to shake them off."

"She shook them off?" Connor couldn't comprehend Donovan's explanation. "What the hell are you talking about?"

"According to Johnson, she went around a sharp curve on one of the back roads and disappeared."

"Where would she go?"

"I was going to ask you the same question. I've made arrangements for someone to check the townhouse and someone else to check the cottage."

"And..."

"Nothing so far. Why would Anne pull a stunt like this?"

"I'm guessing she was sick of being followed."

"Do you have any idea where she might be? You've known her since you were kids. Where would she hide?"

"Anne's safe space, lifetime, has been the Jersey Shore. Somewhere close to Lavallette. That wouldn't be a difficult search this time of the year." He paused. "But, on the other hand, Anne knows every highway and back road from Kentucky to Syracuse. And she's smart enough to know the first places we'd look for her."

"With any kind of luck, we'll be able to track her with credit card purchases. She's sure to get gas, stop at a restaurant, or go to a motel."

Connor sighed, "She's smart enough to have thought about that possibility, too."

Anne

Anne watched the gray Ford and the black sedan speed down Tucker Lane toward Connecticut Avenue. Still wary, she walked back up the hill to her car. For the next thirty minutes, there were no signs of the men assigned to follow her.

A few minutes before six, she started her car, took a left on Tucker Lane, drove up the hill to Highway 108, then turned west, toward Rockville. The Rockville Pike took her to the beltway. She kept pace with the morning traffic on the GW Parkway to Regan National Airport.

Anne backed into a parking space in the long-term parking garage at the airport. She opened her suitcase, exchanged her sweatshirt for a tailored gray jacket, and smoothed her hair.

Once she reached the terminal, Anne got in line at the taxi queue.

"Where to ma'am?"

"Phoenix-Park Hotel."

"Been traveling far?"

Anne laughed, "Yes. I've come a long way in the past few days."

She took her first deep breath when she turned the deadbolt in her hotel room. "I did it." Anne did a little dance around the elegant hotel room.

Connor
November 28, 1989

Connor dialed Donovan's office. "Any sign of Anne?"

"No. You were right. She hasn't used any credit cards. And she probably won't. Anne withdrew a large amount of cash from her bank account last week. All in small bills."

Connor scowled. "I talked to Empañada this morning. His Cartel friends decided to comply with my request. They pulled their guys off the search for Anne."

"They could be lying," Donovan muttered.

"What would be the point? If they want me – I'm in plain sight. They don't have to get her to get me. Let me know if you hear anything."

Connor stared at the phone. *Where the hell could she have gone?"*

He dialed Stuart's work number. "Have you heard from Anne?"

"She had Thanksgiving Dinner at the house. I haven't seen her since then. Why? What's happened?"

"She's taken off."

"Excuse me?"

"Early this morning, she got in her car, drove to Columbia, Maryland, and took the guys who were following her on a joy ride through back roads. She went around a curve and disappeared."

Stuart chuckled.

"What's so funny?"

"Not funny – but also not surprising. Anne was here Thanksgiving and was asking us all kinds of questions. We did everything we could to avoid answering direct questions."

William
November 28, 1989

William drove to the New Carrolton parking structure. *I hope I'm doing the right thing.*

Anne waited near the elevator on the third floor of the parking garage.

"Get in the back seat. How did you get rid of your tail?"

"Took them for a joyride through the Maryland countryside."

William furrowed his brow. "Where's your car?"

"Long term lot at National. I backed in. You have to squeeze between the wall and the car to see my license plate. If anyone recognizes the car, they'll assume I've flown somewhere. With any luck, they'll be confused - for a while at least."

"Connor's worried about you. He called Stuart this morning."

Anne's eyes went wide. "Stuart knows?"

"No, Stuart doesn't know. I feel guilty. He's worried about you."

"You promised not to tell anyone where I am. Not Stuart, not Connor, and NOT Mr. Donovan. Are you sure Stuart won't guess I'm at the estate?"

"I house-sit the estate and take care of the dog when Dot and Randy are traveling. They'll be in Europe for another two months. So, my visits to their house are part of my routine. I've done this for years. I'll go to the estate every day, and I'll stay in the guest apartment over the garage once or twice a week."

William pulled through the gates of Glen Marin.

The house sat on the banks of San Domingo Creek.

Inside, the burgundy and gold of the rich fabrics and rugs complemented the artwork and antique furniture. A legend written in Old English Script over the hearth said it all:

> :earth & aIr & fIre & Water :
> : aLL eLeMents gathereD for a:
> : WeLL of peace at GLenMarIn :

William carried Anne's bag to the guest quarters.

Green brocade wall coverings and creamy yellow chintz curtains gave the room a feeling of welcoming warmth. White wicker furniture and bright white wood trim added to the room's ambiance.

A window seat overlooked the back lawns and the deep-water dock.

Reflection of the sunlight playing on the creek rippled across the ceiling.

Connor
November 30, 1989

Connor couldn't keep his mind on Port Authority Business.

He paced the length of his office – returned to the window wall – turned and walked back again. "Where the hell is she?"

Angela stood at the door, holding several documents for his review. "Where the hell is who?"

Connor stopped and turned. "Anne."

"Dr. Anne is missing?" Angela's eyes went wide.

He sighed. "Yes. Anne disappeared several days ago. No one knows where she went."

Angela thought for a moment, then shrugged. "Last I heard, Dr. Anne is an adult – she's pretty much allowed to go wherever she wants – whenever she wants."

"No – you don't understand," Connor explained as much of the story as he could.

"What haven't you told me?"

"What do you mean?"

"I have a feeling there's more to the story."

"I've told you everything I can."

Connor
Sunday, December 2, 1989

Connor's pager buzzed. He pulled the device from his pocket. *Donovan.* Relief and dread washed over Connor as he dialed.

"What's up?"

"Anne's back."

"Back? Back where?"

"She pulled into her garage at the townhouse about twenty minutes ago."

"Do you know where she's been?"

"Nope."

"Is she okay?"

"She seems to be. All the men could see was her driving the car. Looked like she was alone."

"But…"

"Gotta go. Another call's coming in."

Anne
Sunday, December 2, 1989

Anne dropped her suitcase at the foot of the stairs. I guess I better call Donovan and let him know what I've decided.

"Hello Mr. Donovan. Unless you've changed your mind, you've got a new recruit."

Fifteen minutes later, she carried her suitcase to the second floor. The phone startled her. She threw her bag on the bed and answered the call.

"Where have you been?" Connor's voice was strident. "I've been worried about you."

"Really? Were you worried? How hard did you look for me? I thought you guys could find anyone."

"Where were you?"

"I'll keep that bit of information to myself. I might want to run away again."

His sigh of frustration came through the phone line loud and clear. "Are you okay?"

"Never better. I had a good week. I'm rested and relaxed. I've made some decisions."

"What kind of decisions?"

"Oh, I guess it's something *you* haven't been briefed about."

"Briefed? What are you talking about?"

"Oh, nothing. I'll tell you the next time I see you."

"Damn it, Anne. I can't get down there at the drop of a hat."

"Well, then you'll just have to wait. God knows I've spent enough time waiting for you."

Connor
December 15, 1989

Connor looked out from his office window in the World Trade Center at the lights of the city. The beauty of the nightscape from his office on the sixty-fourth floor filled him with awe. Across the harbor, the Statue of Liberty held her torch high.

His usual Christmas melancholy was overwhelming. It happened every Holiday season—a holdover from all the Christmases in lonely and dangerous outposts.

His direct line rang.

"Quinlan."

"Connor, this is Donovan. Glad you're still there."

"And a Merry Christmas to you too, Mr. Donovan."

Donovan moaned.

"Merry Christmas, Connor. We still have a few days to go. It's only the fifteenth."

"I should have expected your usual bah-humbug holiday spirit. How long do you plan on staying grouchy?"

"Sorry." Connor's voice lightened. "What did you want to tell me?"

"I called to let you know things have changed in Panama."

"Changed? Paul Garcia and I went over Noriega's indictment. The Justice Department has more than enough evidence to convict. The trick will be getting him out of Panama."

"We've been able to start to close down much of the drug operations coming through Panama."

"I thought you called because something new happened."

"The Panamanian National Assembly just appointed Noriega chief of the government and named him Maximum Leader of National Liberation."

"That's one way to spit in the eye of Endara and the United States."

"They added a final nail in the coffin."

Connor waited.

"They've declared Panama's at war with the United States."

"When are we going in?"

Donovan was quiet for the better part of a minute.

He won't answer the question. Something's happening.

"What about Kurt Muse? He's still in Modella. If something big goes down, they're likely to kill him."

"Mr. Muse's plight was brought to the attention of the very highest authorities. They'll do their best."

"What's next on my agenda?"

"Your contacts with the Japanese shipping industry may be of use. The Yakuza are getting overly ambitious. They're expanding their influence from Indonesia to the States. Put it on the back burner. We'll talk after the holidays."

"Can't wait."

"You deserve a short rest. And, you'll have time to visit the pretty doctor. Tell her I said hello."

"Anne? Probably not. I have no plans to get to Maryland or DC anytime soon."

"You haven't been to see her?"

That doesn't happen to be any of your business. Connor took a deep breath to calm his anger. "The Yakuza. I know them well. Mean sons of bitches."

Connor put the phone in the cradle and glanced down at the city again. *Maybe Donovan's right.*

He picked up the phone and dialed Anne's number. "Hi, Wiggles. Can you meet me at the cottage next Tuesday evening?"

"Last time we talked, you reminded me of just how busy and important you are. And, by the way, how little time you had to – how did you put it – drop everything and run to Maryland?"

Connor winced. "I'm sure it'll be late by the time I get there. Please - meet me at the cottage on Tuesday."

Operation Acid Gambit

Master Sergeant Carson completed the final inspection of his team. *They're ready to go.*

Carson, proud to be a professional soldier, came from the South Bronx. He was the neighborhood's odds on favorite to be incarcerated or dead by his twenty-fourth birthday. At seventeen, a judge gave him the choice of returning to juvie or signing up for the military.

He chose the military.

As far as Carson was concerned, life started when he found his place in the Army. Now, after completing years of training and testing, he was a part of Delta Force.

His team was chosen for a special mission to free Kurt Muse.

Carson and his men rehearsed the details of their mission for months. Finally, they left Ft. Bragg and flew to Eglin Air Force Base in Florida to train using a replica of Modella prison. They rehearsed the details of their mission until it became second nature.

On December 19, 1989, the call came. They were flown to Ft. Amador.

The men were ready to go. They added concussion and smoke grenades to their usual kit.

Their blacked-out helicopters waited.

The ops data on this one better be correct.

Carson ducked under the rotating blades and boarded the MH-6 Little Bird scout-observation helicopter.

*Who could ever imagine I'd be breaking **into** a prison? Operation Acid Gambit. Funny name for a jailbreak.*

Pope Air Force Base, North Carolina
December 19, 1989

Life events changed Luke Murry during his sophomore year at Villanova. He was a well-liked and robust rower on the crew team with a grade point average of 3.25.

His father suffered a massive heart attack and died. Luke was left with two choices; obtaining a military scholarship or dropping out of college and getting a job to work his way to a degree in electrical engineering.

The Army was pleased to give him a four-year ROTC scholarship.

Luke happily accepted the eight-year military commitment in return.

After graduation, he went directly to the Infantry Officer Basic Course, airborne school, and finally ranger school at Ft. Benning, Georgia. He proudly wore the Eighty-second Airborne patch as well as his airborne and Ranger tabs.

Now, First Lieutenant Luke Murry's men lined up in freezing rain to board the C141B Lockheed Starlifter.

I'll miss Luke Jr.'s first Christmas. He sighed—*Merry Christmas to me.*

The timing of their mission was critical.

Murray said a short prayer for his friends in the Army's crack Seventy-fifth Ranger Regiment. *Lord, don't let this weather screw up our take-off.*

Their assignment was the assault on Torrijos-Tucuman and Rio Hato airfields. The Eighty-second would immediately parachute in to secure the area.

On signal, Murray and his men boarded the C141.

Operation Just Cause had begun.

Connor
December 19, 1989

Connor drove his pickup truck south on Highway 301 through the eastern shore of Delaware and into Maryland.

He breathed a sigh of relief.

The radio, tuned to an FM station out of Baltimore, played nonstop Christmas music. Connor sang along. He swung south on to Route 213, took the turnoff to Route 50, and followed the signs to Saint Michaels. It was late evening. Still, he was careful to watch his speed on the empty road.

Soon he was on Route 33. The Miles River was off to his right. He turned toward the river. Gravel crunched under the tires as the truck drove down the lane to Anne's cottage.

The lights were on in the cottage. Anne's car was parked near the house.

Connor carried his bag and a bottle of champagne. He tapped on the door and waited. No answer. He knocked again, then knocked louder.

A few minutes later, Anne opened the door, wrapped in a heavy terry cloth robe. A white towel turbaned her hair. "Sorry – didn't expect you this early. I got here half an hour ago I thought I had time for a quick shower."

Connor leaned down to kiss her cheek.

"Put another log on the fire and make yourself comfortable while I dry off." Anne disappeared into the bedroom.

Connor threw his jacket over a chair. The hearth basket held several logs.

Multiple throw pillows leaned against the daybed's metal frame.

The only sound was the crackle of the burning logs.

The fire and a few candles provided the only light.

"See if you can find some Christmas music on the radio," Anne called from the bedroom.

Connor heard a hairdryer start. He found a station playing Christmas music, then walked to the kitchen, pulled two wine glasses from the cabinet, and popped the champagne cork.

He placed the champagne bottle and glasses on the table in front of the day bed.

Connor crossed the room and looked toward Swan Cove.

The light from a buoy shimmered on the water—it looked like a magic path to Anne's dock. An occasional ripple caught the moonlight.

I've been gone too long.

"Is the music all right?" He asked when the hairdryer turned off. "Perfect."

He checked his watch—a*lmost midnight.*

Johnny Mathis was singing the Christmas Song.

"Sometimes, I wonder if you come down here to see the Miles River or me." Anne's voice was soft and lilting.

Connor turned.

Anne stood in front of the fireplace

She was a silhouette surrounded by a filmy white peignoir.

"Damn, you're beautiful," he muttered

Connor took her in his arms.

"Welcome back, Connor." Anne took a step back, picked up one of the glasses, and held one out to him.

"A toast?"

"Yes," she answered, "A toast to new beginnings."

"New beginnings?" Connor led her to the couch.

"We have some things to discuss. I'm ..."

The music stopped in the middle of 'The Little Drummer Boy.' Connor and Anne turned toward the radio.

"We interrupt this program to bring you a news bulletin. American Forces have attacked sites in the Republic of Panama. Panamanian radio indicates they've had strikes against several airfields and key sites in Panama City. The White House has not yet confirmed the attack. We'll bring you further details as they come in. We return you to your regularly scheduled broadcast."

The last few stanzas of Drummer Boy resumed.

Connor's lips curled into a grim smile. *I hope they got Muse out of Panama.* He turned toward Anne. "What were you saying?"

She reached out. "Never mind. You're here. I don't have to worry about whether you're in Panama. The next time you get involved in some intrigue, you may have me along."

Connor laughed. "Have you along?"

He started to say something else, but she placed a finger over his lips. "The short story is I've closed my practice and accepted a new position."

"You what?"

"I did a lot of thinking on my little vacation."

"Vacation? Is that what you call your disappearance? Everyone was crazy worried. No one could find you. How did you manage to elude everyone?"

Anne tossed her head. "I needed time to think and make a big decision."

"I don't understand what you're talking about."

"Sometime in the future, I'll be a part of your team."

"My what?"

"I guess Donovan didn't think you had a need to know."

"Donovan? What does Donovan have to do with anything? He couldn't find you either."

She laughed. "I'll tell you what I'm talking about, and you can tell me about the Yakuza, later. We've got some unfinished business to take care of." She started to unbutton Connor's shirt.

Epilogue

At forty-five minutes after midnight on December 20, 1989, Operation Acid Gambit began.

Delta Force landed on the roof of Carcel Modella Prison in Panama City. They successfully freed Kurt Muse from captivity.

A United States military force came in by helicopter from the Pacific Ocean and landed on what appeared to be an almost perfect landing zone across from the hotel. As a part of Operation Just Cause, the Eighty-second Airborne Division conducted its first combat jump since World War II. They flew from Ft. Bragg North Carolina, landed on Torrijos International Airport, and quickly secured the area.

Manuel Noriega was visiting his mistress at an apartment not far from the airport on the night of December 20. He eluded capture and eventually sought refuge at the Vatican Embassy. After a standoff, he surrendered and was transported to the United States to stand trial for drug dealing.

Thanks to the work of Paul Garcia and his team, the government succeeded in disrupting drug traffic passing through Panama and was able to track the laundering of drug money through the banks of Panama.

Guillermo Endara, the elected president of Panama, alerted by embassy officials about the impending military operation, was moved to the Marriott Hotel for safety. Endara was restored to power.

Hector Reyes was killed by a rocket from a United States helicopter during the operation.

Felicia Alotto returned to work at the bank. She rekindled her affair with Marcos, the young bank executive. He became a partner in the bank, found an apartment for her away from the Chorrillo. She never understood the implications of the information she delivered to Reyes.

Paola del Rubin became an advisor to President Endara and eventually went on to become a Panamanian television reporter and personality.

Her husband, Luis del Rubin, returned to Panama. He became an executive in the new Panama Canal Agency, created after the Panamanian government took possession of the canal.

Isobel Duarte and her husband, Roberto, successfully ran their shipping company.

Ivan "Ora" Oratchewski returned to Germany and was involved in intelligence operations there until he retired. He still resides in Germany, where he has several business interests.

Stuart and William remained in St. Michaels, MD.

Connor and Anne went on to serve their country.

Author Comments

This book is a work of fiction based on historical fact.

My thanks to the many people who have assisted me with this manuscript: Hugh Welsh and Richard Favella for their expertise; Joseph Badal for his encouragement, patience, and suggestions; Margie Lawson and Jodi Thomas for their outstanding writing courses; KJ Waters, my outstanding Business Manager, for all her help; and my family and friends who have continued to encourage my writing and have been anxiously waiting my next novel.

Historical Note

Manuel Antonio Noriega Moreno was a Panamanian politician and military officer who was the *de facto* ruler of Panama from 1983 to 1989.

He became an officer in the Panamanian army and rose through the ranks. In 1968, Noriega became chief of military intelligence. Noriega consolidated power to become Panama's *de facto* ruler in 1983. From the 1950s until shortly before the U.S. invasion, Noriega worked with U.S. intelligence agencies. Noriega was one of the Central Intelligence Agency's most valued intelligence sources, as well as one of the primary conduits for illicit weapons, military equipment, and cash destined for the U.S.-backed counter-insurgency forces throughout Latin America. The U.S. also regarded Noriega as an ally in its War on Drugs, despite Noriega himself having amassed a personal fortune through drug trafficking operations. Though his U.S. intelligence handlers were aware of this, it was allowed because of his usefulness to the U.S.

He had longstanding ties to United States intelligence agencies; however, he was removed from power by the U.S. invasion of Panama. In 1988, Noriega was indicted by federal grand juries in Miami and Tampa on charges of racketeering, drug smuggling, and money laundering.

Following the 1989 United States invasion of Panama, he was captured and flown to the United States, where he was tried on the Miami indictment. The trial, lasting from September 1991 to April

1992, ended with Noriega's conviction on most of the charges. He was sentenced to forty years in prison and ultimately served seventeen years after a reduction in his sentence and time off for good behavior.

Noriega's U.S. prison sentence ended in September 2007. In 2010, Noriega was extradited to France, where he was sentenced to seven years of imprisonment for money laundering. In 2011 France extradited him to Panama, where he was incarcerated for crimes committed during his rule. Diagnosed with a brain tumor in March 2017, Noriega suffered complications during surgery and died two months later.

Maryland Shrimp and Crab – Serves 4

2 Sticks butter – melted

3 sticks celery – chopped

1 medium onion – chopped

4 oz. chopped mushrooms

½ cup Sherry

1 clove garlic

Salt

Pepper

1 lb. deveined shrimp

½ lb. crab meat

8 oz. wild rice

Prepare wild rice (set aside)

Melt butter in a large pan, add the chopped celery, onion, and mushrooms – cover.

Add sherry, cover.

Add Garlic, salt, pepper, shrimp, and crab.

Cover and cook 5 minutes

Remove garlic clove

Serve over rice

About the Author

Gloria Casale grew up in a small blue-collar town in New Jersey. She earned her medical degree at the University of Kentucky and completed advanced training in Anesthesiology as well as Preventive Medicine and Public Health.

She received training in bioterrorism and bioterrorism response at the United States Army Medical Research Institute of Infectious Diseases and is a recognized expert in the international transport of disease.

Dr. Casale was a consultant to the Division of Transnational Threats at Sandia Laboratory. She has been an invited speaker to members of the United States military, as well as members of various posts association on the topics of bio weaponry and the international transport of pathogens.

She currently lives in New Mexico with her tuxedo cat, Hugo.

Upcoming Books

Gloria Casale offers mystery novels for lovers of spy thrillers. So far, she has published Bioterror: The Essential Threat.

The first book in her second series, Counting Down, is expected to be published in the next twelve months. The series details the lives of ten women from one neighborhood. Twenty-five years later, the women are disappearing one by one increasingly frequent intervals. A serial killer is determined to murder them all.

Gloria is also currently working on An Emergency Medicine Memoir she hopes to have the first of a two to three-part series released in the next six months.

Stay in Touch

Visit Gloria's website here: www.gloriacasalewrites.com/
If you enjoyed the book, please leave a review on Amazon or Goodreads.

Please join Gloria Casale's newsletter for occasional updates on
her work, special sales, and exclusive content.
Sign up here.
https://geni.us/GloriaNewsletter

Follow Gloria on these social media sites:

Twitter: @GloriaCasale
Facebook: GloriaWritesBooks/
Pinterest: gloriacasale/

Made in the USA
Middletown, DE
25 October 2020

22738726R00146